SWEET BETRAYAL

KALI SWEET URBAN FANTASY SERIES
BOOK 6

MISTY EVANS

Beach
Path
Publishing

CHAPTER ONE

Betrayal sat heavy on my mind like the coat of frost that glazed the middle of the street I walked.

The majority of the street lights had been busted out by gangs and juvenile delinquents who lived in the shabby townhouses and apartments on either side.

"Hey, Mamacita," a man called from one of the porch stoops. "You're out of your home territory."

At four in the morning, I'd assumed I'd have the streets to myself. In this part of the west side of Chicago—even though it was officially winter—that wasn't the case.

I barely glanced his way. In my short skirt, thigh-high boots, and leather jacket, he naturally assumed I was a working girl who wandered far from her city street corner.

As it was, I *was* a fair distance from my regular stomping grounds, but I was chasing a *lecaro* demon. Case number one hundred and fifty-one on my Sweet Investigations list and my fifth one to chase down since nightfall. I was cold, hungry, and ready to call it a night, but I also wanted to check this one off my to-do list before sunrise.

I ignored the ill-mannered man and kept walking.

He was not easily deterred. "Dangerous for you to be out here alone."

"The night is full of terrors," I muttered, quoting the Game of Thrones line for my own amusement. I didn't care for the series, but Maddy, my young vampire protégé, was always sending me memes from it.

"What's that?" the man called. I was nearly even with the porch now. "Why don't you come over here and—" He finished in Spanish, but I got the drift when he grabbed his crotch and thrust.

I didn't have time to teach him a proper lesson on manners, and he wasn't bright enough to understand he was playing with fire.

Or a demon, in this case. "Careful," I said, continuing on my way, "or I'll remove your dick and feed it to you."

I should've known he wouldn't let that challenge pass. I heard his footsteps behind me, coming up quickly. A couple more sets joined his, some of his buddies who'd been hidden in the shadows and were itching for a fight.

Pelvis guy cut off my progress by stepping in front of me. He shoved me back, his homeboys closing in around him to form a barricade. "What did you say to me, Mamacita?"

Volante, my whip, squeezed around my arm where she was wrapped, letting me know she was ready for action, too. Her handle slid into the palm of my hand. "I'm not your Mamacita. Move or you'll be dog meat."

A snide grin spread across his face, and he turned to his

friends. "Did you hear that? This little thing thinks she can take me."

All the men chuckled. A variety of weapons appeared in their hands—chains, switchblades, and one even had a baseball bat.

"'This little thing,'" I mocked, "has better things to do than teach you manners. Get out of my way, or I will."

The smile fell from his face, and he took a step toward me. If I'd had more time, I would've played with him and his friends. Made them beg for their lives.

As it was, my demon simply wanted blood, and I was keen to give it to her. I let her rise; the moment his eyes locked with mine and mine went full-on black, he hesitated. My turn to smile. "You should be more careful who you try to intimidate and threaten."

He hadn't attacked me yet, and as a vengeance demon, I couldn't take revenge for myself—only for others. Still, I was happy to defend myself. I touched my ring finger to my thumb, forming a protective bubble, then flicked magic at him with my free hand.

He flew several feet up off the ground and, like a bowling ball, knocked all of his posse down. "Strike," I called, maneuvering around the heap of flailing men. "Stay down, or my next hit will be fatal. "

I was bluffing on that part—as a Bridge employee, I was obligated to save humans, not kill them, even if I found them entirely annoying, or they were threatening me with bodily harm. In general, I prefer helping them since I find them fascinating.

We save what we love, and I happen to love a half-human, half-demon. My connection to Rad Beaumont had influenced my decision to save humans, rather than destroy them, for three hundred years.

That didn't mean I would overlook blatant bullying or cruelty. I moved away, hurrying toward my destination while willing them to stay put.

A pipe dream. Pelvis guy yelled, "I'm not done with you, bitch."

The tang of metal and oil hit my nose—he'd drawn a gun. "Now, you're really starting to piss me off," I said, stopping to face him. He pointed a small black handgun in my direction. "I'm late for my meeting, and I don't tolerate assholes."

Just as he was about to squeeze the trigger, I flicked Volante in his direction. She knocked the gun from his hand, and it hit the ground. Before he could react, I whipped her again, her sleek leather wrapping around his ankles and jerking him off his feet. He crashed to the ground, his head slamming into the asphalt, and he yelped in pain. The others had gained their collective feet. Some came after me, some fled.

"The night is dark and full of terrors, and I'm one of them," I called. "Don't ever bother another woman again, or I'll use this whip to do much worse. Comprende, amigos?"

For emphasis, I snapped the end of Volante at them, like a cowboy herding cattle. Most of them were smart enough to step back. Their leader, however, sat up and flipped me both middle fingers, issuing a string of curses.

My next strike took them off. He screamed again, blood spraying from his wounds as the digits rolled on the frosted ground.

"That's exactly what I'm going to do to your dick," I said, marching toward him.

One of his minions grabbed him under the armpits and boosted him onto his feet. Everyone else had already scattered, and this guy was smart enough to drag him away. The dissected digits lay quivering on the road, and my demon smiled. I could use those digits to bait the *lecaro*.

I'd seen and done a lot of gross things in my lifetime, but I couldn't bring myself to pick up the two fingers and take them with me. I'd find another way to bring down the demon.

I ran toward the address of the hideout the *lecaro* had been using. I hadn't gotten around to replacing my car, an Audi TT that the archangel Michael had damaged months ago. Occasionally, my boss Damon loaned me a Bridge Institute car. The rest of the time, I begged rides from my friends. I'd been so busy since leaving Lucifer Morningstar's service and returning to my private investigation business that I hadn't had time to find a new one. It was one of the things on my to-do list for the weekend.

I had a variety of supernatural magic swirling around in my blood. Tonight, the vampire speed came into play as I hurried through the streets and found the location I wanted.

A certain tingling in my blood told me that Rad was already there. I caught the scent of him—ocean breeze and chaos—and followed its trail until I found him lurking in the back lot of the abandoned Victorian mansion home to nothing but mice and bats.

"You're late," he said.

Talk about a muscled snack that the *lecaro* would enjoy feasting on. Not even the black trenchcoat he wore could hide his massive bulk. He'd drawn the hood over his blond hair, and his blue eyes appeared black as the night.

"I'll make it up to you later," I said, sliding into his embrace and nipping his lower lip with my teeth.

He pulled me against him, pressing my breasts to his sizable chest. "You smell like blood. Were you fighting again without me?"

"Just had to put a few idiots in their place."

He kissed me long and deep, until a fake cough from behind him broke us apart.

Maddy marched to the rear of the house. "Save it for later, bitches. I've got a hot date with my latest Netflix crush. Let's get this over with."

"Strip," I ordered Rad.

A brow arched. "What?"

I reached under his trenchcoat to pinch his side. "The coat and the shirt. You're the bait. The flesh eater will take one look at your massive chest and washboard abs, and that will be all the distraction I need to take him out."

He flinched. "You're serious."

I gestured for him to start undressing. "As only a demon ready for blood can be."

"You just want to get me naked," he teased.

"Well, there's that." I winked. "Seriously, though, this should be a cakewalk. Flash your chest and I'll do the hard part."

He rolled his eyes but slid the coat off his shoulders and tossed it onto a dead bush. Next came his shirt, and I gave him a look of approval. His nipples hardened in the cold air. I tweaked one and scraped a nail down his hard pec and the six-pack I would lick later. "I love it when you do my bidding."

He used the shirt to smack my leg. "We'll see who does whose bidding after we arrest this piece of shit."

"Promises, promises," I taunted, strolling for the front door. "And I'm not arresting him. I'm destroying him."

"Wait." Rad grabbed me from behind, spinning me around. "Damon wants him alive."

"What for? This is one of Lilith's pets that ran loose after we battled it out with her and Michael. JR confirmed it. Those demons get a one-way ticket back to Hell."

Rad shrugged. "The boss said to bring him alive."

I grumbled obscenities under my breath. While I was once again doing more work for myself these days, Damon was still my boss at the Institute. He'd tasked me, Rad, Maddy, and Cole with capturing all the members of Lilith's army still running around Chicago. We'd been methodically hunting them down and sending them back where they belonged, so what was different about this one?

I voiced that to Rad. "What does Damon want with it?"

"Believe it or not, he doesn't share much with me, and I can't read his mind like you can." He glanced at one of the broken windows. "We'd better get this over with before we tip the guy off."

Damon was an archdemon and had planted one of his *psuhke* seeds inside me to create a telepathic link between us. Most of the time, I kept it blocked so he couldn't invade my thoughts. It was rare that he ever allowed his shields to be low enough for me to read his mind, so although Rad kept insisting I could, it was more just a point of contention with him. He was jealous, and no amount of reassurance from me would change his mind.

"You go first. You're the eye candy and my perfect

distraction. I'll sneak up behind him." I didn't add, *and lop off his head*. I could always claim that in the heat of the moment, I had no choice.

Damon wouldn't believe it, but I figured it was better to beg for forgiveness than ask for permission.

The place stunk of rotting meat. With no heat, the interior was as cold as the night outside. Even so, flies gathered in packs, covering mounds of decaying flesh that lay here and there. I stuck my nose in the crook of my elbow, breathing shallowly, as I stayed in the shadows and Rad took center stage.

"Hello?" he called. "Anyone home? I've got some beef-cake for you."

Maddy was covering the back to keep our demon quarry from escaping that way. As I eased down the hall, avoiding the clumps of flies, I came to the kitchen, and the rotting smell grew more intense. My makeshift filter no longer helped.

Rad eased up quietly beside me and shrugged. "Either he's out hunting or he's bailed."

A body was sprawled on the kitchen table, the pale moonlight turning the blood black. The flesh was ripped and torn; muscles had been stripped from the bones. I couldn't tell if it was male or female at this point, only that it had been human.

"Talk about terrors in the night. That's fresh," I said. "Hasn't been gone long."

A blur of white on my left caught my attention. I whirled, ready to start decapitating. Something in a sheer nightgown flung itself against my legs. "Help me," the girl whispered. She was shaking hard, causing her voice to hitch. "Please...help...me."

CHAPTER TWO

"Not expecting that," I said to Rad as I untangled the girl's arms from around me and looked her over. She appeared to be eight or nine years old, barefoot, with a dirty face and matted hair. "Do you live here?" I asked.

I feared the mess on the table might be a parent or guardian. She shook her head, still clinging to my waist. "He brought me here."

I knelt to meet her eyes. "What's your name?"

She hesitated. "Susie."

"How long have you been here?"

"I don't know."

Using my blood-connection to Maddy, I tugged the thread—*come inside.* The girl glanced at Rad. "Aren't you cold?" she asked.

He crouched so that he, too, was on her level. "Big, strong guys like me don't get cold."

Susie glanced back at me. "We need to go." Her eyes flicked upward. "Hurry."

I followed her gaze. "The monster is upstairs?"

She tugged on my hand. "Come on."

Maddy slipped in through the back door. Her eyes widened when she saw the girl. "What in the demon-hunting hell is that?"

"Susie," I said, "I want you to go with my friend Maddy here. She'll take care of you while I handle the monster. He'll never hurt you again. Then we'll find your parents, okay?"

Rad stood and tossed Maddy his keys. "Take her to the Rover. There's a blanket inside. Get her warmed up. We'll join you in a minute."

Susie moved toward him, reaching out one of her small hands to touch his arm. "You shouldn't stay," she whispered.

Her tongue darted out to lick her lips, and earthy demon magic hit me. "No!" I shouted and shot out a hand to grab her by the hair.

Too late. The child morphed in the blink of an eye into the very demon we were hunting. Topping six feet and oozing green pus, the face became an elongated clash of razor-sharp teeth and bulging eyes. Its hands, swinging from ape-like arms, ended in three-fingered claws, and the mass of its upper body dwarfed the side-by-side fridge in the corner.

Rad's magic, along with mine, hit it full force. It screamed and bellowed, but didn't miss when it swung for his gut.

The three claws sank deep and came away with pieces of skin and intestines. Blood and viscera flew, splattering the walls.

Maddy sucked in a shocked breath, and I sent Volante around the thing's throat. Without a command from me, my whip contracted and squeezed hard enough to force the demon to its knees.

Rad staggered, hitting the counter, his guts leaking from his side. The horror of it made my demon roar to life, flashing to the surface. His eyes met mine and caught. Something in them shifted, and then, with the next breath, Rad became...

A full-on demon.

In all the time I'd known him, I'd never seen his demon surface.

But this wasn't his chaos demon—it was a bigger, badder *lecaro*.

The Rad version towered over us, the chest I'd admired earlier becoming three times its normal size. His face contorted into a mirror image of the *lecaro*, and the injury disappeared, instantly healing itself. He cut loose a roar that shook the room and sent Maddy and me stumbling backward.

Great. Now I had two of them.

Before I could use Volante to snap the first one's neck, Rad swung a giant mitt at it. Claws sliced through flesh and bone, taking its head clean off. The gory piece of meat hit the floor with a sickening thud and rolled to my feet.

Rad, looming over me, huffed loud breaths in and out, staring at the mess as the body lost its balance and fell sideways. Raising a massive foot, he stomped down on the head, crushing it. More blood and goo were added to the horror.

Backed up against the door frame, I exchanged a look with Maddy. She cowered near the window and gave me a *what the hell do we do now* look.

Good question. I had no idea.

Volante returned to my arm, but I kept her handle in my

hand. I didn't want to use it against Rad, but I wasn't sure how else to handle him if he came after us. "Rad?"

Dull, dark eyes met mine. They were tiny in such a large head, but they were his. He gave another huff and then, just as quickly as he'd morphed into the *lecaro,* he changed back.

He dropped like a bag of rocks to the floor, an arm sliding through the gore left behind by the crushed head. He didn't seem to care or even notice. He groaned, his bones popping as he returned to normal size. His eyes rolled back in his head.

I rushed to his side, thankful to see the gash in his stomach was still healed. My demon retreated. Not entirely, but enough. I ran my hands over him from the top of his head down to his jeans. I needed to make sure he was once more my boyfriend, and not the monster I'd just encountered.

"Kali," he groaned, clutching his stomach.

"You're going to be okay," I assured him.

"What just happened?" Maddy asked. "*How* did it happen?"

I had no idea on either account. "Help me get him to the car."

Our superior strength was the only thing that allowed us to carry his dead weight. Maddy pelted me with questions, but I had no answers, and finally asked her to stop so I could think. My young protégé didn't appreciate it, but seemed to understand that I was at a loss.

We had to pull over several times on the way because Rad kept throwing up—violently. While I could use my magic to clean up the worst of it, I couldn't do much about the smell. I rolled down all the windows, embracing the frigid night air as I sped to the Institute.

Once we arrived, I got him on his feet, and he revived enough to walk inside on his own. I wanted to take him straight to the infirmary to see Kirill, but Rad refused.

Neve, my human friend and the Institute's office manager, arrived as we were arguing in the outer lobby. "Damon's waiting." Her gaze swept over Rad. "You don't look so good."

He dragged himself to the elevator. "I've been better."

Maddy and I rode up to Damon's office with him. "Dude," she said, "I thought you were half chaos demon."

He leaned against the back panel, eyes closed. His voice was raw. "I am."

"Funny, because you looked like that cannibal demon when you wigged out. Only...bigger and uglier."

He ran a hand over his face. "I don't know what happened."

I wanted to reach out and comfort him, but I didn't know what to say. "We'll figure it out."

A nagging don't-tell-Damon feeling tugged at me. Something was off—big time—and I didn't know what. I didn't like the idea of revealing too much to our boss until I had an explanation.

Unfortunately, I had a witness—Maddy—no *lecaro* to pony up, and an ill enforcer who wasn't bouncing back as quickly as his injury had. This mission had gone all kinds of sideways.

As we headed for Damon's, I murmured to the others, "Let me handle this."

Maddy gave me a dubious glance, but said nothing.

Although I didn't want the title of Vampire Queen of the Chicago House, I had it. I was her sovereign, and she was duty-bound to follow my instructions without question.

Rad said nothing. I wasn't sure if that was because he understood my concerns or if he was afraid he might vomit again if he opened his mouth.

Damon was writing something as we entered, and he didn't look up. I motioned Rad to the sofa, and Maddy stood near the bookcase. Taking the lead, I strode to Damon's desk. I reeled in my impatience while he took his time with the paperwork and set down his pen. "Report?"

"The *lecaro* demon has been taken care of," I said.

He barely glanced up at me. "Is it in the dungeon?"

"No, it was sent back to Hell."

He picked up the pen and stabbed it into the holder. "I requested it be returned to the Institute."

"We ran into an issue." I didn't offer more. "I had no choice but to destroy it."

Maddy coughed and then tried to hide it by clearing her throat. "It tricked us. We thought it was a girl, and then..." I gave her a *shut-up* look, and she turned away, suddenly interested in a painting Damon had on the wall.

"Explain," he barked at me.

"There's not much to say." I stood stock still as if I had nothing to hide. Rad slouched on the sofa, head back on the cushion. "It blindsided us, then it attacked. I had no choice but to decapitate it."

He eased back in his chair, his gaze scanning me, Maddy, and Rad in turn. A slow, silent reckoning that made my skin crawl. "How did it trick you?"

I forced myself not to fidget. "It appeared to us as a

young girl, like Maddy said. She begged us for help. Then, she morphed into the *lecaro* and attacked Rad."

My boss's intense, dark eyes slid to my boyfriend, zeroing in on him. "Are you in need of medical assistance?"

Rad tried to sit forward, swayed, and gripped the arm of the couch to steady himself. "No."

What a liar.

Damon knew it. "Why do you look as if you've been poisoned?"

"About that," I said.

"It's nothing," Rad growled.

And then he shot off the sofa and barely made it to the trash can, where he promptly vomited what was left in his stomach.

Maddy groaned and covered her mouth as if she might lose it, too. I covered my nose and turned away.

Damon didn't so much as blink. "I take it the demon touched you."

Rad braced his hands on the edge of Damon's desk, continuing to stay bent over the trash. He didn't seem capable of answering at the moment, so I did. "The thing gouged out a piece of his stomach. It's healed now, but he's got lingering side effects."

Damon waved a hand, and the contents of the can evaporated. Thankfully, so did the smell. "Present yourself to Kirill and have him administer the proper medicine to counter the poison."

I grabbed Rad's arm to guide him to the door. I was more than ready to escape. He needed to be checked out—and the sooner the antidote went in, the better.

Damon stopped me. "Kali, stay. Maddy, assist Rad to the infirmary."

She screwed up her face and hitched a thumb toward the exit. "I'm needed at Carpathia. Dru has work for me."

Chicken. She was giving Rad a run for his money in the liar department.

Damon picked up his pen and a stack of papers. "The Chicago House will carry on quite well without your ten-minute delay. I'll let Master Alexandru know you'll be late."

Busted. Her eyes went wide, and as she looked at me for help, I handed Rad to her. "I'll handle it. Go."

She rolled her eyes and took him by the elbow. Disgruntled, he tried to pull away, but she kept a firm grip on him as she half-dragged him out.

The moment they reached the hall, Damon used his magic to slam the door shut. I looked longingly at my exit, then turned to face him. "What's up?"

"I'm waiting for you to tell me the rest of the story."

I kept my face neutral. "There is no 'rest of the story.' We cornered the demon; it turned on us."

He looked up from his task, his intense irritation pinning me to the spot. "You expect me to believe that a lowly *lecaro* demon ambushed you?"

It was highly improbable, but what could I say? "Shit happens sometimes."

"Is there something else you want to tell me?"

"About tonight? Right before I arrived, I had a run-in with some lowlifes on the west side, but I handled the situation. Other than that, I've been working my ass off to close these cases and get Lilith's army contained."

He didn't give any quarter. "You should be able to handle twice that caseload without breaking a sweat."

Who was busted now? *Yep, this vengeance demon, who had angel essence and vampire blood in her system.* "Are you dissatisfied with my work?"

"I'm dissatisfied with your withholding of information."

I was walking a fine line, but continued to play dumb. "Am I supposed to turn in my daily itinerary to you? Do you need to know how many espressos I've had? How many times I cursed at downtown traffic?" I shrugged, acting confused. "What exactly do you think I'm withholding?"

Nothing about him changed except for the minuscule flare of his nostrils. He was smelling me.

Ever since the rooftop incident where I'd taken a trip into the void—a place outside of this space/time reality—and met an entity called an Omni, I smelled different. It wasn't detectable by everyone and barely so even by those who could pick up on it. I'd insisted to anyone who asked that it was from Michael giving me a piece of his essence to assist my fight against Lilith that day.

To avoid being obliterated, I'd fought it—and ripped off a piece that now lived inside me. That fragment carried a strange power and intelligence called The Unknowing. Its attributes were unlike anything that existed on Earth, hence the moniker.

According to Michael, there were four Omnis. The entity that humans, angels, and demons called God was one of them. Each of the others was an equally incomprehensible type of power. Timeless, immortal, and extremely dangerous.

One of my father's texts, written long before I was born,

claimed the Omnis were the origins of all existing supernaturals. According to the text, God stole fragments from each of the others to stop their destructive nature and turned those pieces into artifacts.

Being a creator, He hid the artifacts on Earth and then covered the Earth with His creations—humans. The injured Omnis needed to be whole to wipe out dimensions, and they were consuming souls to fuel their hunt for those artifacts.

Those of us in the know believed one was hiding in plain sight. According to Michael and Lucifer, it was the archdemon currently interrogating me.

Possessing a piece of that timeless and immortal power might allow me to locate the artifacts—if Damon didn't get to them first.

We needed to destroy them to prevent the Omnis from obliterating everything and erasing the existence of all souls, planets, stars, and dimensions, yet I couldn't wrap my mind around what exactly The Unknowing wanted.

Damon and I had shared moments of friendship, and I'd thought I could depend on him. Not for everything. Not like Cole or Rad, but for a lot of things, nevertheless. He knew my past. He'd stopped my demon from ruining me. He'd given me a reason to live after Queen Maria had destroyed everything and everyone I loved.

But now, I knew why.

He'd been *grooming* me.

That was the term Michael had used. I'd never suspected a thing. How could I? I'd had no knowledge of such beings. I'd never experienced the void. Had never heard of The Unknowing.

"Kali?" Damon's voice snapped me out of my ridiculous and ill-timed reverie.

Time for me to outdo Rad and Maddy in the lying department. "I'm still trying to manage the angel essence. It's...weird." *Real descriptive, Kali.* "It makes me feel off one day and riding a high like nothing I've felt the next. I'm not hiding anything—I'm just dealing with my issues, okay? You don't need me bending your ear about it. Besides, it's not like you can help. No one can help me."

He opened his mouth as if to argue, but the door flew open. Michael strode in, throwing his arms wide and grinning. "There she is. I thought I felt you in the building. Miss me, sweet demon?"

Topping seven feet, with flowing golden hair and a body that filled out the clothes tailored for him like—well—like they were made for him, he sucked up all the air in the room. His angel presence made my skin crawl, yet the essence he'd put inside me was at war with it. That part of me wanted to fall at his feet like his biggest fan.

His timing was perfect. He'd probably been eavesdropping. I had to play it cool. "What do you want, *porca miseria?*"

Calling him a miserable pig didn't faze him. The two of us had gotten good at our roles. His was to irritate me. Mine was to hate him. It wasn't a stretch of my acting skills.

He winked. "I've been training with Cole, and I need a break. I'd like to go to Sweet Investigations and talk to Sophia about Lilith."

Sophia was my online computer assistant, and it was a solid excuse to get us both out of the building. The only problem was that I didn't want to leave Rad. "You just want to hit on Di again."

Aphrodite was my best friend and the Goddess of Love. Yep, *that* Aphrodite.

He made prayer hands in front of his chest. "You found me out. She *is* hot. Do you think she likes me?"

"If you so much as—"

"Out!" Damon barked.

Our act had worked. I didn't need to be told twice.

"Kali," he said before I made it to the door. "We'll continue this discussion later."

I gave a mock salute, shoved the giant angel into the hall, and closed the door behind us.

CHAPTER THREE

"Where are you going?" Michael asked as I headed for the stairs to the infirmary.

"To check on Rad."

He shot me a disgruntled look. "We need to talk."

That was code for *we need to leave the Institute*. We couldn't discuss Omni business this close to Damon without fear of his eavesdropping. Even the great archangel wasn't sure if his wards could keep an Omni out.

"And we will as soon as I make sure my boyfriend is okay."

I took the stairs two at a time with him on my heels. When I got to the next landing, I whirled. "Why don't you wait for me in the parking garage? I'm not sure how long I'll be, but I'll find you when I'm ready."

"You mean like you did last week when you took off with Cole to get ice cream, rather than discussing the latest chapter I translated in your father's book?"

Oops. "It's not like I want to spend time with you." That

was the truth, but I added a wink to let him know I was still in character, just in case anyone was listening. "And there's nothing in my father's book that'll help me round up the loose demons in Chicago. Until I have that under control, whatever you're uncovering will have to wait."

He winked back, accompanied by a gesture that wasn't quite as friendly. "What's wrong with your boyfriend?"

"Wish I knew." Another truth. What we couldn't say out loud was still expressed in creative ways. I gave him a classic rude Italian hand gesture. "He was injured and turned into the same type of demon as his attacker. He's back to normal now, but it left him exceptionally ill."

He motioned for me to go through the door. I wasn't getting rid of him, dammit. I flung it open and marched down the hall. His footsteps were silent, but I felt his angelic mojo pressing against my back, heavy and suffocating. *The sooner we get this over with, the sooner we can attend to more important matters.*

Another byproduct of his angel essence—it was as if I could read his mind. I didn't get word-for-word monologues, but his thoughts were apparent. Scary, that.

No one was in the infirmary except for Rad and Kirill. The scent of antiseptic and bleach hit my nose as we entered. Rad was in a hospital bed with multiple machines hooked up to him. There was a steady chorus of beeps and whirring. His eyes were closed, and his breathing shallow. On the rolling table next to him was a kidney-shaped vomit pan, a carafe, and a paper cup.

Kirill studied one of his monitors, frowning. I tried not to take that as a bad sign—the Pestilence demon was always frowning unless there was food around. "How is he?"

He glanced up, slightly startled, and shook his head, making his fleshy jowls jiggle. Rising from his rolling stool, he came around the table to cast his gaze on his patient. "Outside of elevated blood pressure, he seems normal. Hard to tell with chaos demons, though. Their 'normal' is abnormal for the rest of us."

'The rest of us' being angels and non-chaos demons. The three of us stood in a line, watching Rad.

"That's useless," I said, pointing to the vomit pan. "If he upchucks, you're going to need a—"

Rad's eyes bugged out, and he heaved over the side of the bed. The disgusting results splashed all over the floor and the IV pole's wheeled base.

Point made.

With a sigh, Kirill donned gloves and grabbed tweezers and a plastic bag. Michael and I watched as he gathered samples from the vomit and then made the rest vanish with a few words.

Rad lay back in the bed, rubbing his stomach and groaning. I offered him water, and he drank it; then he asked for seconds. He gulped that, too, and drifted back to sleep.

After depositing his bag on a table with assorted lab tools, Kirill ditched the gloves and worried at his chin between his thumb and finger. He motioned me to follow him to his office. Inside, he fumbled through a stack of files and brought out a notepad. "Rad described the incident for me, but I'd like to hear your take on it."

Michael crossed his arms and leaned on the door frame. "Me, too."

I relayed the story again. "Have you ever heard of anything like that happening before?"

Kirill was the closest thing we had to a full-fledged doctor. "I've seen and heard a lot in my time." He scribbled notes on the pad. "But no, nothing like this. A half-human, half-chaos demon doesn't suddenly morph into a *lecaro*."

"Not even if the *lecaro* poisoned him?"

Kirill shook his head. "There's no poison." His gaze drifted to his lab and the bag waiting for tests. "At least none that I've discovered so far."

"Is it possible he's not a chaos demon?" Michael asked.

"No," Kirill and I responded in unison.

"It's rare enough that Rad's part human," Kirill continued. "In general, the human body isn't strong enough to contain chaos-level magic. The fact that he's held it together this long is a testament to his control. In the time you've known him, Kali, has he ever shifted into his chaos demon?"

I shrugged. "We've been apart for most of our relationship, but I've never seen it."

Michael snorted. "Three hundred years, right? Not much of a relationship, is it?"

I flipped him the bird.

"All the times he saw you about to die, he never morphed?" Kirill asked. "Seeing you in extreme danger never triggered it?"

I shook my head. "Never."

"I...never...have," Rad croaked from the bed.

We filed back out and hovered around him. "Never?" Kirill repeated. "Odd, but probably the reason you're still alive. A full morph could be too much for your human half to handle."

He could barely keep his eyes open as he stared at me. "Why would an attack by the *lecaro* trigger it?"

I looked at Kirill, who shook his head. "We don't know," I told him. "How are you feeling?"

One hand rubbed his gut, the other his head. "Like I've had the flu for a week straight."

"Your vitals are normal, outside of some elevated blood pressure. This should wear off soon." Again, I glanced at the doctor. He gave a hesitant shrug. I proceeded to sound confident. "We need you back in the field, so no slacking, okay?"

He didn't give any indication that he knew I was joking. I patted his leg through the sheet and motioned Kirill to follow me to his office. Once there, I closed the door behind us, Michael taking a seat on the desk. "He is going to get better, right?"

"No clue," Kirill said. "I'll examine the sample and see what it can tell us." He pointed toward his microscope. "The thing is, the *lecaro* might have simply been a trigger for whatever this is. Even for the supernatural, the laws of nature in this dimension demand that there is order to keep the chaos in check. I suspect that whatever order has kept Rad's demon from taking over has been disrupted. It's...failing." The look he gave me suggested I brace myself. "The only thing we can do is figure out what that is—what is the order that can keep his demon at bay."

I didn't like where this was going. "How do we do that?"

"I'll know more after I do a full tox screen and dig into the research on chaos demons," he replied. "That's all we can do for now."

The way he said it didn't give me much hope. "What happens if we don't figure it out?"

Kirill offered a chastising grunt. "What do you think

happens if the chaos takes over? We won't be able to get him back."

"What does that mean?" Michael asked. "If the chaos takes over."

I marched to the window between the rooms. Rad was out again, his chest rising and falling in shallow gasps. "He'll be full-on demon. It'll destroy the human side of him. All of it."

"It will kill him," Kirill confirmed. "And the chaos side will have to be sent to Hell. It's the only place capable of containing such an entity."

Michael slid up beside me, whistling softly under his breath. "Looks like you'd better work fast."

My heart felt like a red-hot poker had been shoved into it. I had no comeback. Not even a rude gesture for him. I set my shoulders and flung open the door. "Keep me posted," I told Kirill.

Michael jogged after me. "We still need to talk."

We did, but I had more important things on my mind now. "I'm heading to my office. If you want to talk, you can ride with me, but once there, I expect you to work."

He made a face as we raced down the fire stairs. "Work?"

"I have a lot of cases right now. This will put me further behind." I hit the underground parking garage and headed for the Land Rover. "If you want to talk, that's the deal."

"Fine." He gave a dramatic eye roll. "What about Maddy?"

"What about her?"

She popped out from behind one of the support beams. "Right here. And Cole's on his way."

"Cole?" I stopped at the driver's door. "Doesn't he have training?"

She was watching a video on her phone and smacking gum as she climbed into the back seat. "Damon thought you might need help now that Rad's sick."

Help or a watchdog? Michael and I exchanged a look. We couldn't discuss Damon being an Omni if we had company.

Cole wasn't there yet, and I could drop Maddy at Carpathia on the way. "Get in," I ordered the angel.

Michael folded himself into the passenger seat, and I took off.

"What about Cole?" Maddy asked.

"I'll catch up with him—" I slammed on the brakes as the War demon appeared in my path. "Or not."

Maddy snickered. Michael gave an annoyed huff. Cole climbed into the back. "Leaving without me?"

"I'm in a bit of a hurry." I glanced in the rearview mirror. "Rad's in bad shape. I need to figure out why and how to reverse it."

He tapped the back of my seat. "Sophia might know."

I accelerated, wheeling off the Institute grounds and into traffic. "I sure hope so."

CHAPTER FOUR

Maddy refused to be dumped at the House. Her on-again, off-again boyfriend was waiting when we got to Sweet Investigations. He wanted some time with her, so they went down the block to the coffee shop.

One down, two to go. I handed Michael a case file. I preferred to do things digitally, but he didn't own a cell phone. Every time he got too close to a computer, his divine energy fried it. "This couple has an entity in their house that's scaring their daughter," I told him. "It's one of two things—either a poltergeist or a demon. My guess is the latter since the haunting seems to have started only recently."

The archangel glanced over the single sheet of paper, scanning both sides. "A ghost? That's what you want me to take care of?"

"If it's a spirit, cross it over. If it's a demon, send it to the Pit. Should be a simple, straightforward resolution, either way."

His hulking form filled my office. His wings fluttered with irritation. "Will they be expecting me?"

A seven-foot guy with wings? Not hardly. "I recommend you tone down the archangel vibe. I realize there's not much you can do about your height, but you need to hide the wings and lower the attitude." I rustled through my top desk drawer until I found one of my cards, handing it across the desk to him. "Show them this, tell them you're new and you don't have your own business cards yet. Do your best not to frighten them or the girl any more than they already are. They're human. At least, mostly. The mom has a bit of Scottish witch ancestry, and that's how she knows about me and what I do."

His face lit up. "I'm getting business cards?"

Gods, no. "Let's see how this goes first."

He tucked the card into a pocket and tossed the folder on the desk. "I don't exactly know how..." He shuffled his body weight back and forth.

I waited for him to finish, but he didn't, eyeing the exit. "Don't know how to what?"

Cole strolled in with a cup of coffee in hand, heading for my couch. He removed a few of his weapons before slouching down on the cushions and sipping his beverage.

Michael flushed, his pale skin turning an unusual shade of pink. "You know." He flapped his arms awkwardly. "Handle a case. I've never done any of this before. Shouldn't I go through some kind of official training or something?"

I rocked back in my chair, enjoying his embarrassment. "Right. My bad. I assumed because you're an angel that you would know how to handle spirits and demons." I mean, it wasn't out of the realm of possibility, even if he hadn't spent time on Earth. "If it's a poltergeist, tell it to go to the light. If it gives you trouble, call Neve. She handles these types of things all the time. If it's a demon, you should be able to blast it with your magic." I made an explosion gesture with both hands. "Poof."

He frowned. "You really want me to handle this on my own?"

He was normally so arrogant it surprised me he was resistant to the idea. "You can take Cole with you."

They both looked at me as if I'd grown a second head. Michael held up a hand, heading out. "I've got this."

Once he disappeared, Cole straightened and downed the last of his coffee. "Why do I feel like you're trying to ditch me?"

Now that Michael was gone, I didn't need to. "Sorry." Even though it wasn't heartfelt, it seemed like a good idea to pretend I was. "I'm worried about Rad."

The War demon motioned at the large screens on the wall. "Ask Sophia for help."

"Good morning, Master Cole," my virtual assistant said in the sexy voice JR had programmed her with. "How may I assist you today?"

Cole loved it when she addressed him as such, and a rakish grin spread across his scarred face. "Guitar boy has lost control of his demon," he told her, "and we need a way to fix him." He eyed his empty cup. "And I need more coffee."

While Sophia understood demons quite thoroughly, we spent twenty minutes going back and forth with her, trying to find more insight into what had happened with Rad. She kept telling me that my basic premise was flawed—that it wasn't a demon-specific problem; it was a *chaos-order problem.*

"Natural systems learn from and evolve with their environment to exhibit both structural order and dynamical chaos," she explained. "They are fluid states, each existing in the other."

"Huh?" I asked.

"Yin and yang," Cole said.

"Yes, Master. Dualism. In philosophy, order comes from the rational mind and represents stability, structure, and comfort. Discipline, scientific theory, and any way to understand sequences and classes also fall under order. Chaos arises from the creative self and represents unexplored territory and possibilities. It's where new ideas form, but it also generates randomness, unpredictability, and erratic motion."

She spent a great deal of time trying to get us to understand chaos theory with regard to philosophy, economics, the universe, and even something as insignificant as carbonated bubbles from a poured soda.

Some of it made sense, but a lot of it seemed...irrelevant. I didn't care about the butterfly effect or the three-body problem. We weren't dealing with carbonation or the universe. We were dealing with a demon, and we needed a solution.

Vicky DeClement, a vampire-witch hybrid I despised, blew into my office while Sophia highlighted perverse inevitability, a tangential axiom of Chaos Theory. Since my brain was whirling in circles, I almost welcomed the interruption. That was saying something since I hated the witch.

"You've done nothing to help me," Vicky complained, pounding a fist on my desk. It had been over a month since her last entanglement with her mentor, Lilith, and that had left her a crispy piece of coal.

Her hair was growing back, and her skin no longer showed signs of the third-degree burns she'd received, thanks to her vampire blood, but she still lacked eyelashes, which gave her eyes an odd, bug-like appearance. "You promised me revenge, and you're sitting here talking to your computer."

"I assure you I am more than a computer," Sophia replied. "I am a digital assistant that uses voice recognition and—"

"Shut up," Vicky yelled.

While Sophia wasn't human, I wasn't about to tolerate Vicky's rudeness. "If you wish to discuss your case, make an appointment," I snapped. "And FYI, every demon I pursue in the Chicagoland area right now is a lead to Lilith. Crawl back into your hole and let me work."

"Lilith is in Naperville," Sophia volunteered. "At your compound."

I came out of my chair. Cole shot to his feet as well. "Why didn't you tell me that?" I asked her.

"Your question was about Chaos demons."

I rubbed my forehead, ignoring Vicky's smirk. Lilith was at my compound, which had originally belonged to Raj Nudra, a former vampire king I'd eliminated. I'd acquired his assets as spoils. "How do you know this? Who spotted her?" I asked.

"She posted on social media, calling her followers to her," Sophia responded. "I have access to the surveillance cameras at the compound. Would you like to view her?"

Cole swore, automatically beginning to check his

weapons and ready himself to go with me and hunt her down. "Yes," I responded. "Bring up the surveillance."

A dozen screens came to life, showing me the interior rooms of the mansion, garage, and grounds. I didn't see Lilith in any of them, but there were a few cars in the drive. Apparently, her followers, or just the curious, had decided to join her there.

"Not good," I said. "Whoever shows up will be turned into a sacrifice, or possibly lunch."

"I'll call my team," Cole said, dialing his phone.

"I'm coming with you," Vicky said. "I'll make sure she doesn't get away."

"We can't just go rushing in there," I told her. "We need a plan."

She punched the top of the desk again, this time denting it with her superior strength. "You're chickenshit."

I grabbed her by the wrist and jerked her forward so we were face-to-face. "Of the two of us, I'm the one who didn't end up fricasseed the last time I went head-to-head with her. If you want to handle this, by all means, do so. I'll be happy to clean up your ashes when it's over."

She ripped her arm out of my grip and hissed at me. "You're fired!" Then she stomped out of the office.

I wasn't sorry to see her go, but it didn't change anything —she might not be my client now, but I still had to send Lilith back to Hell where she belonged. Everyone was counting on me to do that, only now, I wasn't getting paid.

Cole pocketed his phone. "Damon says to stand down. He's putting together a strike team."

"Bullshit. You and I are the strike team. Has he forgotten that?"

Cole grinned. "My guys will be there in fifteen minutes, maybe twenty, depending on traffic. We'll meet them."

Time was running out. I wanted to focus on Rad, but this couldn't be avoided. I had Lilith within my grasp.

Although I never spent time at the compound, I'd been there enough since it had become mine to know its layout. That gave me the upper hand. If I could capture her and return her to Lucifer Morningstar, I'd get a gold star and get him off my back.

I could send Cole's team alone, but they wouldn't have enough power to handle her. They needed me to bag her.

I considered my options. "Have your Merc demons surround the place, while you and I infiltrate. I'll handle Lilith. You take care of anyone else inside."

"And Damon?"

I'd worry about him later. "Let's get there before his strike team does."

Cole headed for the door. "I like the way you think."

Vicky was no doubt on her way right now. I yanked open one of my desk drawers to grab my favorite cherrywood stake, hoping I had a chance to stab her in the heart during the fight.

What I saw inside made me pause. "Uh, Cole?"

He was beside me in a heartbeat, staring into the drawer over my shoulder. "Satan's balls. What the hell?"

Someone had left me a present. In the drawer next to the stake was a heart. While no longer attached to its owner, the bloody organ still beat as though it were. *Thud thud. Thud thud. Thud thud.*

The landline on my desk rang, and Sophia answered. "Sweet Investigations. How may I help you?"

Through the speaker, I heard Kirill's voice. "Kali's not answering her cell phone. Is she there? This is urgent."

My stomach fell. I snatched up the landline receiver. "What is it? Is Rad..."

I couldn't say it.

"Still alive, but he's been losing his normal form. Damon's moving him to the dungeons."

"*Dungeons?*"

"They're strong enough to contain him temporarily. If you've got a better idea, tell me how to keep him from going full-Chaos demon on us. I'm not sure how much longer he has before..." *we have to put him down.* The words hung in the air like an anvil poised to drop.

Dammit. Lilith would have to wait. So, too, would the beating heart inside my desk drawer. Kirill was doing me a service, giving me a heads-up so I could at least see Rad one more time. "Don't do anything until I get there."

I hung up, and Cole asked, "What about Lilith?"

"She gets to terrorize Chicago for another day unless Damon's strike team can handle her."

"I've trained that group. It's excellent, but containing Lilith requires a whole different level of magic."

I was already heading for the door. "Which is why Damon himself will be leading them. You coming?"

He stood his ground, an expression on his face that made my stomach clench even tighter. It was his *we're walking into a no-win situation* face. "Do you think you can save him?"

Deep down, I was terrified of the answer. "I have to try."

He pulled the keys out of his pocket. "I'll drive."

CHAPTER FIVE

Damon's strike team was pulling out as we pulled in. Inside the Institute, I raced to my apartment and grabbed Rad's guitar and pick from where he'd left them.

"What's that for?" Cole asked, jerking his chin toward the instrument.

"Our only hope," I said.

"I don't think Guitar Boy is up for a concert."

Cole's phone went off. He screwed up his haggard face. "Damon wants me to meet him and his team."

As I'd predicted, Damon had left with them. I was surprised he was willing to order Cole away and leave the Institute so unprotected. Maybe I was simply overly paranoid, but there was very precious cargo in the private bunker these days. Angelic cargo in the form of Lucifer, his wife, and his child. No matter how many wards we had or types of magic that could repel various types of attacks, removing himself and his best warriors from the premises was a tactical error.

Cole knew it, too. Still, if I was here, I could hold off the worst of any attack until help returned. "Go. I'll handle this."

He pulled another of his infamous faces. "I'm not leaving you on your own with the Chaos demon."

"Damon won't be happy."

His reply suggested Damon do something to himself. While I preferred working alone, Cole had always had my back. I didn't admit it to him or anyone else, but I liked having him around. It was almost a relief that he was refusing a direct order from our boss because his loyalty was with me.

He was armed to the teeth, so there was no need for me to hand him my favorite punch dagger. The weapon with a T handle could be concealed in his closed fist, the blade extending between his fingers. I handed it to him anyway. "Stay alert."

Understanding the gesture was more a sign of thanks than a reflection of my concern for him, he accepted it with a curt nod. We both knew if he gutted my boyfriend, he'd be on my shit list, but we also both knew that it was better to be prepared for any outcome.

Kirill met us at the entrance to the dungeons. The magical security barriers and wards were thick and constantly shifting. They held poisons and spells designed to keep the prisoners in and those unwelcome out.

These days, I wasn't sure which side of that line I fell on. Walking around with a piece of Omni inside me could land me in one of these cells.

Because Rad was my blood slave, he felt my presence as soon as I entered and passed through the layers of security. He was dressed and sitting on a cot, looking far too pale and wrung out. Standing on shaky legs, he staggered toward me and gripped the iron bars containing him. "Kali." It came out as a wheeze, purple bruises smudging under his eyes.

Humans, even a hybrid like him, always amazed me. How they survived in this world, how they continued to hope. To create music, paintings, and technology from nothing more than imagination and creative thinking.

"You're on your feet," I said, giving him the most encouraging smile I could muster. I wrapped my fingers around his, propping the guitar between my legs. "That's a good sign."

He shook his head. "Kirill says there's no cure. This is probably my last hurrah as something resembling human."

I glanced back at the Pestilence demon. "Open the door and let me in."

He shook his head, his jowls jiggling. "Can't. Damon's orders."

That was the reason the weasel had left. He knew I'd insist on trying to save Rad myself, and he refused to risk it. "So he's not man enough to stay here and take me on over this." I shook my head in disgust. "Give me the keys and get out of here. I'll tell him I snuck in. You won't be blamed."

Kirill rolled his eyes. The top of his partly bald head shone under the harsh glare of the lights, and he sucked on his gopherish front teeth. "He'll call bullshit. You can't sneak in here without me knowing it. Plus, he put everyone on high alert, because we all know you'll try exactly that."

"Why does he care?" I flipped him off in my mind, hoping it was paying attention. "It's not like I'm trying to sic Rad on the world so he can wreak havoc. I just wanna go inside his cell and comfort him."

Kirill's bushy brows rose. "Flowery language from such a tough demon."

Rad slid his fingers out from under mine. "Damon's right. It's too risky." He slunk back to his cot and flopped down, throwing an arm across his eyes.

"Most of us are soldiers," Cole said. He tilted his head toward the archdemon. "Even if some have more significant powers." Then he tilted his head at me. "You're something beyond that. A force multiplier. Losing one of us would be a problem for Damon, but he would overcome it. We're replaceable. You? Not so much. You're one of a kind. Losing you could cripple the Bridge Institute and everything he's worked for."

Damon didn't put anything ahead of his commitment to the Bridge. At least, that's what I'd always believed. If he was an Omni, though, his commitment took on a new meaning.

Seraphina, one of the *vitiums* who carried the vice of envy and was Kirill's sometimes girlfriend, came running into our midst. Her turquoise eyes were lit with excitement. "I think I've got something."

"What?" Kirill and I asked in unison.

Sera was a healer and had seen her fair share of disease and death. Before this current Amazon warrior meat suit, she'd been the infamous Florence Nightingale. "The spinal fluid sample—there's an anomaly."

I flinched. "You extracted his spinal fluid?" A horribly painful process and one I couldn't believe Rad had bounced back enough from already to be able to stand.

"That and bone marrow," Kirill informed me. "Standard operating procedure."

Sera launched into a more clinical explanation. "Cerebrospinal fluid analysis and cytomorphological examination are central diagnostic parameters when it comes to—"

I stopped her with a raised hand. "I got it. What did you discover?"

"Removing that sample of spinal fluid may be why he's conscious and moving around," Sera said, nodding her head. "The extractions also removed a portion of the anomaly, thus allowing his magic to fight back."

Rad sat up, hanging his arms over his bent knees. "So all you need to do is drain my spinal fluid and remove all my bone marrow, and I'll be saved?" The sarcasm in his voice was vicious. "Gee, sign me up."

"I have another idea," I told him, "but I want to see this anomaly first."

He shrugged and flopped back down on the cot. "Whatever."

I turned to Sera. "Show me what you found." She and Kirill headed up the steps, and I pulled Cole back so they wouldn't hear. "Get the keys. I'll be back."

A nod. "Better hurry, or I'll off the whiner before the chaos takes him."

"I heard that," Rad said.

Cole grinned. He was purposely riling Rad up to keep him fighting. I gave him a grateful smile.

Inside the lab, Sera stared through a microscope, adjusting a knob. She shifted it aside and pointed for me to look through it. "Check it out."

I slid into her vacated spot and did so. Through the lenses, I found myself looking at a bunch of blobs on a glass slide. Some were perfectly circular, while others were oddly shaped, and they all moved as if alive. "Are these cells from your samples?"

"Lymphocytes and monocytes. White blood cells. An increase in lymphocytes is often seen in viral infections—"

"You said it wasn't a virus," I said to Kirill.

"It's not a standard one," Sera told me."Keep watching."

On the slide, the moving cells tangled with each other, some doing a bumper car routine while others absorbed their counterparts like piranhas. A particularly aggressive cell devoured three in a row, Pac-Man style, then shuddered.

In the blink of an eye, it turned an inky black and ballooned up to nearly cover the slide. A black hole sucking in all the other cells.

"What the...?" I whispered.

"I've never seen anything like it," Sera said on a reverent exhale. "It's truly an anomaly. Unprecedented." She sounded far too excited about it. "We may have discovered a whole new disease."

Kirill shooed me aside and took over, examining the slide. Sera let him get a gander at that one, then traded it out for another.

Meanwhile, I felt a clawing sensation in my stomach. I knew that blackness. That void.

Except, it wasn't even a void. It was a blackness thick enough to smother you. The Unknowing. I'd known without a doubt when I fought it that it wanted to consume me, just like that cell on the slide. Not to simply exterminate me, but to remove me from existence. My entire life. Total annihilation, as if I'd never existed.

I staggered, turning away from them and leaning against

a nearby counter. I braced my hands on the top, forcing myself to take deep breaths.

While I had fought the Omni and absorbed a piece into my body, it hadn't seemed to affect me in any way.

Now, I realized how wrong I'd been.

I'd poisoned Rad with it.

Somehow, someway, the essence of that thing had gotten into his body. A death sentence.

Not just death—*obliteration*.

My gut cramped. That's what The Unknowing did—it removed things from existence. Wiped them out entirely.

Rad wouldn't simply die. I—we—would cease to remember him. We would have no recollection of his ever being here.

A sob escaped my throat.

"What's wrong with you?" Kirill asked.

I'd made a pact with Lucifer and Michael not to tell anyone about the Omnis or my encounter with that one. I couldn't explain to Kirill and Sera about what they'd discovered without breaking that pact.

Yet, not warning them about it might sentence them to the same fate as Rad. Those cells might jump hosts as easily as fleas.

The only positive was that I wasn't contagious, outside of sharing bodily fluids. Rad probably wasn't either. He was the only one showing any adverse effects, so I had to assume the rest of the people I'd come into contact with were still safe.

Rad was my only blood slave these days since I'd weaned off both Vicky and Arman, and Tabriss was gone. My blood was the most likely means of transmission, but I couldn't rule out sex. Luckily, again, Rad was my only partner.

When faced with overwhelming odds and a crisis I had no idea how to handle, I buckled down my emotions and channeled Damon. Ironic, no? But he was the one who'd taught me how to handle any and every situation. He'd modeled how to lead under disaster, plight, upheaval, and hardship.

Don't get emotional. Don't take it personally.

My vengeance demon code.

I straightened and faced the two pseudo-doctors with calm steel in my veins. "Quarantine those slides and the samples. I'll need to test both of you and make sure you're not contaminated." I strode out to the emergency alarm and held a shaking hand over it.

Both Kirill and Sera startled, firing off questions. My only answer wasn't one they wanted to hear. "The Institute is in lockdown until further notice."

I pulled the metal lever.

An alarm sounded, and lights flashed. The infirmary door latched with an audible click, locking us in.

CHAPTER SIX

Locks can't keep out the devil.

Outside the lab, chaos erupted, and none of it was due to Rad's magic. To my knowledge, the Institute had never been forced into a lockdown before, and I could hear running feet, shouts, and pounding on the outer door. The phone began ringing off the hook.

Before I could explain to Kirill and Sera that I suspected whatever was infecting Rad had potentially infected them as well, Lucifer appeared in front of me. "What in the fires of Hell?"

The king of Hell is formidable in the way that only a fallen angel with a giant chip on his shoulder can be. His absolute beauty—chiseled jaw, dark eyes, raven-black hair—was sometimes hard to take in. It engulfed every room he entered.

Considering he was the leader of demons, he commanded respect and deference from us, no matter the situation. My demon came to attention and wanted to throw herself at his feet.

Since the two people he cared most about lived in the secure underground bunker at the moment in order to avoid Lilith's threats, it didn't surprise me that the lockdown sent him looking for me.

Kirill and Sera stopped shouting long enough to drop their gazes and bow their heads to him.

I lowered my gaze but didn't bow my head. "You know that, uh, *private* matter we've discussed before?" I asked. "I think my boyfriend may be infected with it."

Lucifer blinked once, processing my coded message. "How is that possible?"

I gave a noncommittal shrug. "I'm guessing in one of the usual manners—the sharing of bodily fluids."

His full lips pressed together with a hint of disgust. Apparently, thinking about Rad and me doing the nasty icked him out. "I seriously doubt that's how it works."

I addressed Kirill. "Show him the slides."

Kirill and Sera led him past the infirmary beds and into the lab. While Sera escorted him to the stool and he peered through the microscope, I explained. "Rad was attacked by a *lecaro* demon this morning and had an unusual reaction. He became the same type of demon, morphing into an exact replica, only twice its size. Sera discovered these black cells in his spinal fluid."

Lucifer studied the slide for a long time as Sera prepared a fresh one. Kirill hooked a cord to the microscope, and a view of the slide's contents came up on a laptop screen nearby.

We all watched as a series of inky-black cells attacked

healthy ones. Ninety percent were devoured within a minute.

"I fear Sera and Kirill have been infected since they've been handling these samples," I said. "I can't take the chance that the only form of transmission is...you know."

For the first time since I'd become personally acquainted with Lucifer, he seemed speechless.

Coming off the stool, he bore down on me. "Let's find out."

Before I could ask what he was doing, he gripped the back of my neck. A lancing pain shot down my spine and locked up my entire body.

My eyes bugged out. Drool ran down my chin. I lost control of all of my limbs, which jerked and trembled like live wires.

The pressure on my skull was so intense it made me scream, but my throat was as locked up as my spine, and only a high-pitched whisper escaped my lips. My vision whited out, leaving a dozen black spots—like the carnivorous cells—writhing and spinning in whirlwinds.

Lucifer released me, and I staggered back on jelly legs, hit a stool, and tumbled to the ground with it in a loud clatter. He faced Kirill and Sera, and they both stepped back.

His magic froze them in place before he gripped each in the same manner. They, too, spasmed, their eyes rolling up in their heads as their bodies became trembling rag dolls.

His hold on them lasted less time, and they dropped to the floor in two puddles when he released them. Their limbs twitched, and drool ran from their mouths. The three of us sat blinking at each other as he towered over us.

"You are infected. They are not," he proclaimed. He spoke to Kirill. "Shut off that annoying alarm."

Kirill staggered to his feet, swaying like a drunk. He hit the doorframe and exited, while Sera took great gulps of air and gripped her stomach.

"Could you excuse us for a minute?" I asked her.

Eager to get away, she nodded and used the lab tables to steady herself as she trailed after Kirill. The alarm fell silent, and I got to my feet to shut the door so I could speak to the angelic asshole in private.

"This is good news, right?" I gasped, still trying to process the violation of my body.

It was always impressive how much he could convey without moving a muscle. Disgust and annoyance oozed from his pores. "That your mate is infected with the essence of an unknowable entity because you didn't take precautions?"

I leaned against the bench where the laptop showed the last healthy cells had been obliterated. "I had no way of anticipating such a thing." I rubbed my queasy stomach and swallowed down bile. "The good thing is, we now know Damon isn't an Omni."

He tilted his head slightly, quirking one dark brow. "How so?"

"Because if he were, he would've infected his wife and the other lovers he's had. Well, maybe not the goddess Nyx, because she's a goddess, but the others were demons. None of them showed signs like Rad has, so that means Damon is just an archdemon."

"Omnis possess an undetermined kind of power. He could have prevented himself from infecting them."

I deflated. "I suppose that could be true, but..."

"What are you going to do about the Chaos demon?"

I rubbed my forehead where a throbbing headache had taken up residence. It wasn't every day that you had your spinal fluid analyzed by an archangel's magic and lived to tell about it. "I am open to suggestions. If I can't stop those black cells from devouring his healthy ones, he's going to die."

Lucifer sighed in exasperation. I wanted to call him a drama queen. "You must find a way to remove them from his spinal fluid."

Sure, I'll get right on that. "Because that's super easy."

As per normal, he didn't appreciate my snark. His magic slapped against me, reminding me of exactly who he was and nearly knocking me off my feet. Initially, the fact that I carried Omni essence had scared him and Michael. Since it hadn't manifested anything of consequence, their apprehension about me using it against them had waned. "You carry the same cells inside of you, and they are not destroying anything. Figure out why, and you'll figure out how to save him."

I had to bite my tongue. If I knew how to do that, I wouldn't be panicking. "If you were in my shoes, and it was Amy who was facing obliteration, what would you do?"

That gave him pause, although it didn't lessen his obvious irritation at me. He hated it when I turned the tables on him. "I would extract her spinal fluid and replace it with a clean version."

Again, piece of cake, right? "How?"

"First, I would try commanding the Omni cells to return to me. If you have any power over them, you should be able to direct what they do."

Okay. That was smart, and I should have thought of that. "Like being head of the Chicago vampires gives me power over them."

A nod. "If that fails, direct your doctor to remove the spinal fluid and allow Rad's body to regenerate a fresh batch. Since he's partially human, the cerebrospinal fluid and cells should regenerate in eight hours or so. Once no Omni cells live in his blood or other tissues, he should regain full health."

I didn't know anything about this stuff, but it sounded good. "How painful will that be for him?"

Lucifer walked to the door, done with our conversation. "I imagine quite."

He left, Kirill and Sera giving him a wide berth. I rubbed the back of my neck, trying to figure out a way to call those cells back to me. I should've asked Lucifer how to do that. In the meantime, I needed to get Rad out of the Institute. He might still be a danger to others and to me, so I had to find a secure location. The only one I could think of wasn't in this dimension.

I'd already taken Rad to Michael's alternate realm once to explain what had happened to me in The Unknowing. I'd determined it was the only safe place I could fully disclose what was going on without fear of Damon eavesdropping on the conversation.

But before I dropped Rad into another type of prison, I needed to make some accommodations.

Still feeling wobbly, I forced myself into Kali mode and blew past the others on my way out.

"Hey," Kirill called. "Where are you going? You have some explaining to do."

I stopped only long enough to say, "I need to handle the critical situation with Rad first. When I'm able, I'll explain as much as I can. For now, quarantine the slides, and keep this between us."

He was about to argue. Then seemed to remember that Lucifer was part of our group and decided that if I ordered secrecy, it might be in his best interest to follow that request. Kirill was smart enough not to want to go up against Lucifer.

He gave me a sour face to let me know he disliked being bossed around, but Sera touched his arm and nodded. "Take care of Rad. We'll contain the slides and keep our mouths shut."

I gave her a grateful smile.

Kirill had the last word, though, making it a threat. "For now."

It was the best I could do. I turned and hit a wall of scowling archdemon. I staggered back. "Damon," I said, mentally chanting, *merde, merde, merde!* I'd been hoping to avoid him for obvious reasons. "You're back."

His black tactical gear matched his hair—and the eyes snapping at me in anger. "Explain."

I started to skirt around him. "False alarm. I thought whatever had infected Rad might be contagious." My voice rose as I tried to sound super positive. "Turns out, it's not."

I never do 'super positive' Kali voice unless I'm hiding something.

And he knew it. He grabbed my arm before I could escape. "We need to talk."

The last thing I needed—or wanted. "Rad is still in danger of dying. I have two possible ways of saving him, but I'm running out of time."

"That will have to wait." He pushed me out the door and down the hall toward the elevator. "My office. Now."

CHAPTER SEVEN

My voice rose in frustration. "Do you want Rad to die?" I tried to wrench my arm away, but Damon's grip was an iron vise around my bicep. "I don't have time to talk."

He dragged me into the elevator and, with his magic, hit the button to the office floor. His body blocked me in as effectively as the four shiny walls around us. "You're not going anywhere until you tell me what you're hiding."

To avoid his interrogation, I needed to go on the offensive. "I could ask the same of you."

He stepped back. Blinked. "What are you talking about?"

Offensive move number two. "Did you capture Lilith?"

He narrowed his eyes at my attempt to redirect the conversation. "She was gone by the time we arrived, but she left you a message."

By the look on his face, I knew I wasn't going to like it. "What?"

The elevator stopped, and the doors hissed open. "Your servants have been beheaded. A note left on one of them said your head would be next."

Merde. "They weren't servants." They weren't friends, either—just leftovers from Nudra's reign. They'd come with the mansion.

Still, I felt responsible for them. They'd been loyal employees. Granted, their loyalty was because I'd filled their former boss's position rather than actual devotion, but their deaths still upset me. "I should've warned them."

Even though we hadn't moved, the elevator doors closed. Damon used his magic to stall it as we faced each other down. "It's unlike you to be distracted and forget something of such importance."

He was right. It was an *errore colossale. My* colossal error in judgment. "And their deaths are on me. I'll inform Alexandru and see what penance is made to their families."

"I'm rather surprised your hunt for Lilith has taken a backseat to your other cases."

He was blaming this on me? "Those cases are directly linked to her. They are the best tracking devices to find her."

"And yet, you've closed many of them, and she still walks free."

As does at least one Omni.

Was I trapped in an elevator with it?

Damon was in some kind of mood, that was for sure. While I couldn't complain that we weren't having this conversation in his office, where he held all the power, the close quarters of the elevator made it feel like torture. At least in his office, I had room to get away from him physically, if not mentally. Here, it felt as though he had me pinned against a wall.

I was under a microscope, his gaze and magic probing deep. I fingered Volante, calming myself as best as I could. The only sure way for me to gain the upper hand was to stay on the offense. "You haven't been yourself since you came back from Hell," I said. "What's going on with you?"

He'd taken the question about Lilith in stride, but this seemed to leave him speechless. His brows drew together in confusion.

I continued. "You've been even more sullen than usual. Withdrawn. Confrontational if something doesn't go your way. We recently saved demonkind and stopped a horrible prophecy from coming true. I'd think you'd be a little happier."

His magic rose, his smoky wood scent enveloping me to the point of making my throat itch. The elevator doors opened on his silent command, and he pivoted, walking out and leaving me behind.

O-*kay*.

My comment had hit a sore spot. A part of me considered hitting the button for the ground floor and fleeing, but I knew that would only anger him and he'd simply hunt me down and force me to have this conversation all over again.

Trailing after him, I continued. "What happened when you were working for Lucifer directly to hunt down the Fallen?"

His office door swung open as he approached. "Nothing."

One word that told me something significant *had*

happened. I'd only been guessing. I hesitated before following him into the room. I stopped in the doorway. "You know you can confide in me."

An electrical buzzing came from my left. "There you are," Neve said, approaching in her wheelchair. "I've been searching all over for you. What was with the lockdown?"

She was rocking a Stevie Nicks look today in a long skirt, gauzy shirt, and black hat. "I thought there might be a contagion in the lab. Everything's cool, though. Why are you looking for me?"

She held out two slips of paper. "Michael's been calling. He's in trouble. Why did you send him to handle a poltergeist? You should've called me."

We'd been through this before. Keeping her inside the Institute kept her safe, and although she *was* a ghost-whisperer, poltergeists were a nasty bunch. She had skills when it came to handling them, but I preferred she didn't tangle with the supernatural since she was human. "He's an archangel. He should be able to handle it on his own."

"Well, he can't. The thing is out of control."

Damon joined us, exasperation coating his voice. "You gave Michael an assignment?"

"He wanted something to do," I said in my defense. "I thought he could handle a simple haunting."

"I can assess the situation and see what needs to be done," Neve offered.

"No," I said.

"Do it," Damon countered.

She stuffed the slips into my hand. "The other message is from Cole. He said he has an 'exploding tomato' in the dungeon. He needs your help, ASAP."

An *exploding tomato* was our personal code for 'bomb.' It rarely meant a literal bomb; we used it to signify a magical one.

Rad.

I took off.

Damon called after me, "What's going on?"

I swung into the elevator the moment the doors slid open. "Something bad."

Before I could hit the down button, he was filling the space with me again. We rode in silence, the short distance seeming to take forever.

The elevator only went to the ground floor, so we raced down the steps to the dungeons. He never ran anywhere, and yet stayed close behind me.

Before we got to the cell containing my boyfriend, I could hear yelling, growling, and the sound of splintering wood. Rounding the corner, I came upon Cole, leaning back against the wall across from the bars, arms crossed. While he appeared unconcerned, his War demon magic was thick in the air, creating a barrier between him and Rad.

"About time," he said.

"Is he losing it?" I asked.

He jerked his chin toward the cell. "See for yourself."

As I turned with trepidation to see what was going on with Rad, Damon grabbed my arm.

My breath caught in my chest.

The bed had been shattered into pieces. The mattress had been ripped apart, the foam guts scattered across the floor. The entity inside wasn't Rad. A giant figure loomed in the far corner, its head down and shoulders bowed, too tall for the ten-foot ceiling.

Completely naked, the curvaceous monster beat its fists against the walls, leaving dents in the concrete. Long, dark hair covered much of its back, hanging to its waist in thick strands that looked familiar.

Magic rippled under its skin and roiled out, filling my head with pressure and tickling my inner demon. She sat up at attention, curious and wary, greedily sucking on the earthy taste of it. On my arm, Volante squeezed.

When I caught a flash of the faint tattoo on the side of the monster's neck, I froze. The matching one on my own had faded to a delicate silvery spiderweb of lines and whorls, but I'd recognize the unique design anywhere.

Because I was the only one who wore it.

That's when the realization of what—*who*—I was looking at sank in.

"Satan's balls," Damon swore.

As the thing raging in the cage sniffed audibly and glanced toward us, I had no words. Even my extensive collection of curses deserted me.

Alert to the danger in the face staring at us, my inner demon roared to the surface, ready to defend and kill. A protective shield automatically formed around me, and my magic flooded the area, only adding to those already in place.

The naked monster locked its gaze on me, its pitch-black eyes an exact replica of mine. Facing us, it moved with lethal grace to the bars full Monty. Large breasts swayed, and the hips shifted left to right as it advanced. Its hands wrapped around two of the bars.

I'd never been overly modest, but I felt entirely exposed to my boss and best friend.

Because...that thing? Rad had morphed again—into me.

My giant twin parted her full lips in a grin. Her tongue shot out to lick them as it sized me up. "Hello, sweet *alciscor*," it purred in a sultry tone that was my voice. Only this was a level of evil I rarely embraced. "I've been waiting for you."

CHAPTER EIGHT

Alciscor.

Volante's handle slid into my palm.

Lilith was the only one who ever called me by that ancient name.

I squeezed it tightly. Was she possessing Rad? Had the *lecaro*'s attack and subsequent sickness left him open to her magic?

As a demon, she could enter a human's body and take control, but she was far too powerful for them to handle. She also found humans disgusting and beneath her. One of the most prideful of all of us—maybe even more so than Lucifer —I couldn't imagine why she would possess Rad in order to confront me.

Or why she was imitating me.

Mind games. She did enjoy those. Was this all that was? Had she used Rad's human half to take over his body so she could...what? Freak me out? Force me to face myself?

With half a thought, I stepped forward. "My Queen," I said, using the term she preferred. "What may I do for you?"

"*Queen?*" Cole spat out.

At the same time, Damon caught me around the waist and pulled me back, keeping me from getting close enough for Rad, aka Lilith, aka *me*, to touch.

"Let me go," I growled, my magic repelling his.

His power wrapped around me like a steel grip, lifting me off the floor. "Even with the extra wards on that cell, it's too dangerous," he snapped, his breath warming the shell of my ear.

My demon surged, and all the mixed-up magics inside me fueled her. She snapped his hold like it was nothing. He grunted, surprised, and tried to grab me again. She deflected his effort with a wave of black magic that nearly knocked him down.

That's new.

Volante left my arm and flicked the tip of her whip at him. Feet once more on the stone floor, I adjusted my jacket. "Get Salmad. Tell him we need an exorcism."

Damon, furious over being rebuffed, but still the smartest and most sensible out of any of us, nodded at Cole. The War demon hauled ass to a spot a few feet away, taking out his phone and punching buttons.

"This doesn't mimic possession," Damon said under his breath, spite thick in his tone. "How can you be sure?"

My doppelganger watched me with increasing intensity. Spikes dug into my brain as if Lilith were a mountain climber clawing her way to my innermost thoughts.

I triggered a fresh surge of power to knock her away and slammed down a barrier between us. Volante was eager to snap at her, but I gave the whip a mental command to retreat. Reluctantly, she slithered back into place around my arm. "I agree it's atypical, but she's the only one who uses that term for me."

Cole murmured into his phone. Damon paced in a half circle, eyeing Monster Kali on the other side of the bars. "Why take your form?"

How the hell did I know? "Why don't we ask?" I stepped toward Rad, keeping just out of reach. "My Queen, why use the Chaos demon to speak to me?"

A low chuckle, half-growl, emphasized her next words. "He is your only weakness."

Not the only one, but the biggest. My brain flipped through options. I still needed to save Rad. "I have a proposal for you."

She tilted my head. "You have a vengeance contract out on me from the vampire-witch hybrid. I don't think I'll care for your proposal."

I smiled as if I knew something she didn't. "One witch's vengeance is the Mother of Demons' opportunity."

Another curious twitch of her head. "I'm not going back to Hell."

"Leave Rad alone, and I won't need to send you there."

The chuckle this time was definitely a growl. The menace in it suggested she wanted to fillet me over an open spit. "You aren't my endgame."

Interesting, because it sure seemed like it. "Then who? Lucifer? Aren't you tired of trying to best him?"

Even more interesting, the eyes that matched mine locked on me as if Lilith were *avoiding* the actual subject of her attention.

Which made me turn to look at Damon. "You."

He didn't so much as flinch. "Why would Lilith come for me?"

Yes, indeed, why would she? "Care to hypothesize?"

It was rare for Damon to shrug. He did so now, appearing completely unconcerned. "I have none."

I peered at Rad again. "Why him?"

My likeness seethed, showing her teeth, then inhaled deeply. "Can you not smell it? The potency?"

Archdemons exuded power, vigor, and virility. After being around Damon for so many centuries, his natural potency had little effect on me, except when he wanted it to.

Lilith breathed deeply again, a blissful look washing over my stolen facade. "I know you do. You thrive on it, don't you, *alciscor?*"

Damon cleared his throat. "She's playing games."

She was, but I wondered why. Her distraction was taking us off track. "You've had plenty of opportunities to engage with the archdemon. You've never shown interest in him before. Why now?"

She still refused to look at him. "His power will help me to—"

Sal appeared. "What do you want?"

A few months ago, I'd eliminated Tabriss, the Fallen angel he'd been in love with. He continued to be furious at me over it. I didn't blame him—I would have felt the same way if the situation were reversed—but I found him to be one of the most annoying supernaturals I had to deal with. I had little patience for his attitude. "Lilith is possessing Rad. I need you to exorcise her."

"This is no typical possession," Damon added. "I've never encountered one like this."

Sal was carrying his beloved Bible, but he didn't bother to crack it open. He gave both of us the stink eye. "Is that all I'm worth to this place anymore?"

I fought hard not to roll my eyes. "Your insight would be appreciated." I motioned for him to step closer so he could see into the cell. "Out of all of us, you're most likely to have a solution for this problem."

Although his expression remained cold and detached, he strode forward to check out Rad. Upon seeing the metamorphosis that my boyfriend had become, Sal hastily backed up and made the sign of the cross. "*Spiritu Sancto*," he whispered.

'By the spirit' was as close to a swear from the priest as he was likely to issue, yet the shock on his face said it all.

"Yep," I replied. "Lilith has somehow infected Rad with her own shapeshifting ability and is now donning my likeness."

"The Lord save us all," Sal said.

His words held a bit too much spite for my liking. "Can you exorcise her or not?"

"This is most unusual." He fingered the edges of his worn book—a nervous habit. "I can try, but no guarantees."

The Queen of Hell chuckled softly from my lips. "Save your breath, priest."

And just like that, Rad's body locked up, his head snapping back and throat exposed and straining. All of my features melted away, leaving his in their place. Black smoke streamed from his open mouth, evaporating into thin air. He collapsed to the floor, unconscious, and I shoved Sal aside to rush the door.

Damon reached for me, his fingers only able to brush my arm as I sidestepped him. He wasn't stopping me this time.

The wards, however, did.

Frustrated when I couldn't open the door, I sent a pulse of my magic into the bars, floor, and ceiling. The streams flashed out of me, lighting up the space as if I'd flicked on a hundred floodlights.

"That's new," Cole said with the bite of shock in his tone.

I didn't just bring down the wards. My juiced-up magic incinerated them, along with the iron bars. When the light winked out, all that was left were piles of rusty metal at my feet.

Rad groaned. I ignored what I'd just done and hurried to his side.

A new voice rang out in the dungeons. "What is going on now, Kali?"

Lucifer had joined the party.

He stomped past Damon and Cole, glaring at me as I knelt beside an unconscious Rad. I paid him no mind, frantically patting and shaking my boyfriend. "Wake up, dammit. Come on, Rad."

His body spasmed, and his back arched. I didn't know where to grab him, how to hold him, as his entire frame shook from head to toe in the grips of a ripping convulsion. It ran up and down his body in waves, and I tried to send my magic into his system to calm it.

"Explain," Lucifer demanded.

"Kind of busy here," I shot back.

"First the lockdown, now this. You are upsetting my wife. You are causing earth tremors, even in the bunker."

Rad jerked again, bowing off the ground. His jaw was clamped, and I tried to work a piece of my whip between his teeth, afraid he might break them or swallow his tongue. "I could give a flying fuck about disturbing you. I'm trying to save a life here."

Lucifer's magic snapped out, smacking me aside. A blanket of it fell over Rad, instantly calming him. As I righted myself, I stared at his now relaxed form, breathing easy.

I breathed easier myself, seeing the distress wiped from his expression. He still wasn't conscious, but at least the convulsions had stopped. "Thank you," I said reluctantly, shifting back to kneel beside him.

"I'm still waiting for that explanation," Lucifer said.

Our onlookers grew, Kirill and Maddy joining Cole, Sal, and Damon outside the cell. "Lilith was possessing him," I told Lucifer.

"Lilith cannot penetrate the Institute," he said with utter confidence.

"It was an abnormal possession," Damon stated. "She somehow used the Chaos demon's human side to infiltrate his being."

I ran a hand over Rad's side where the demon had carved out a chunk of skin and tissue. The wound had closed up, only a set of raised scars remaining to show where those claws had ripped into him. "She didn't access him the normal way," I said, hovering my hand over the spot and sending a magical probe into the area.

"What are you doing?" Maddy asked.

"Searching for the implant Lilith's minion left behind."

"Implant?" Damon echoed.

Like you did to me with your psuhke seed, I replied telepathically.

Everyone watched as I slid my hand above the area, inch by inch. Nothing.

I slowed my movement even further, circling the wound again. It had to be here. It was the only explanation.

There. The slightest prick.

Barely moving my fingers, I lingered over the spot, tickling it ever so slightly with my magic. Like a fine sliver from a cactus that's impossible to see without a magnifying glass, it nicked me. "I've got it." The question was, how did I draw it out?

"Got what?" Kirill asked.

I sent a look over my shoulder. "We tested him for physical viruses, but not for magical ones. The *lecaro* demon left a barb in him, so thin none of us noticed. It's connected to Lilith."

"How?" Maddy asked.

I slipped my magic around the elusive sliver and latched on, trying to pull it out. It slipped from my grasp. "Like an antenna," I told her. "It receives and transmits. She can possess whoever it's embedded in for short bursts."

Damon spoke to Kirill and Sal. "Have you heard of such a thing in all your studies?"

Both shook their heads.

"How do you know this," Sal asked with an accusatory tone, "if none of us have ever heard of it?"

How did I? Was it the Omni essence inside me giving me insider information? "Oh, come on. This isn't that unusual. Plenty of demons and other supernaturals can cause disease and illness. They can inject viruses and spread bacteria. Archdemons can force their *psuhke* seeds into others." I didn't bother to glare at Damon. "This is simply a different form of imprinting."

"Is Lilith listening to us right now?" Maddy asked.

I nudged the sliver again. This time, I turned my magic into a sticky piece of tape and adhered it to the wafer-thin fragment. It didn't seem to have sentience and didn't fight me, but it was embedded deep, the scar tissue that had formed around it securing it tightly, even though it wasn't a physical thing.

Sweat ran down the side of my face. I folded my sticky magic around it and firmed it down. Then I gave a tug.

It slipped right through my magical fingers.

I swore loudly, the Italian words echoing off the ceiling and walls. Lucifer brushed me aside. "Let me."

"It's so thin and wispy," I said, drawing back my hand. "You can't—"

A wave of his fingers over the area, and a cloudy shard of energy emerged, suspended over the wound. It was no bigger than a hair and wiggled like a worm.

"What do we do with it?" Kirill asked.

Good question.

"I have an idea," Damon said. "Get a magic-proof container."

Kirill hustled off to do so.

"I'm no longer needed," Sal said. "I shall return to the chapel to my prayers from which I was so rudely interrupted."

My impatience exploded inside me. Before I knew my

feet were moving, I'd crossed the expanse and slammed the priest into the wall. "If you're so put out by us, why don't you leave?"

He blinked in surprise, but slowly, his wide eyes returned to normal. He wasn't frightened of me, only annoyed. "Maybe I will," he said.

Cole grabbed my arm. "Let him go, Kali. He's not worth the effort."

I did, giving Sal a push toward the exit.

"What's with you?" Maddy asked under her breath.

"Rad was possessed and nearly died. Excuse me if I'm not Mary Sunshine at the moment."

She patted my shoulder. "Will he be all right now?"

I glanced at him, still lying unconscious. Would he? Mary Sunshine raised her head, full of hope, but a part of me knew better. "I don't know," I whispered.

It felt like they were the hardest words I'd ever had to say.

CHAPTER NINE

"Will he?" I demanded of Lucifer.

The fallen archangel stared down at Rad, unblinking, as I marched back inside the cell. The sliver of whatever Lilith had put inside him wriggled in the air like a tiny silver tapeworm with minute hooks at each end. "It would be wise to keep him contained until we can further assess the damage."

I studied Lilith's intrusive barb, the silky sliver seeming to come to attention under my scrutiny. It slowed its movements and shivered, the hooked ends turning to face me. "If she was possessing him, why did it turn him into a mirror image of me and that *lecaro*?"

"Unknown," Lucifer said. "She has dabbled in many areas of magic since the beginning of time. I suspect this is simply another concoction of hers."

A shapeshifting concoction that threatened to throw everything into chaos. I needed to get to the bottom of it. "She knows I'm hunting her, so she brought the fight to me. Quite brilliant." I shot a glance at Damon. "But she said you were her game. She wants your power to do something. Any clues as to what?"

He'd been staring at Lucifer, and his black eyes slid to me. "I told you, she's playing games."

"Could be." She was definitely known for that, but her interest in him had seemed genuine. "She's tried taking out Lucifer, Amy, and the baby to no avail. Maybe she wants your magic to boost hers so she can finally achieve her goal."

Lucifer crossed his arms, both annoyed and tired of the conversation. "That's not enough power to overthrow me."

Damon seemed affronted. "How do you know?"

The archangel didn't like being questioned. "You are a powerful demon, and you could certainly increase her abilities, but in this room? You are the least powerful of all of us. If she were truly interested in finding a source to assist her, she would not bypass Kali."

Damon's gaze snapped to me again, assessing, before it shifted to Lucifer. "What have you done to her?"

Damon! I feared for my boss's well-being if he continued to question the archangel like this. His tone alone, not to mention the confrontational energy pouring off of him, was about to get him sent to the deepest level of the Pit. *What are you doing?*

Lucifer quirked one of his dark brows. His angel magic flared bright, and I flinched back, waiting for another of those slaps. "Watch yourself."

Damon stood his ground. "Or what?"

Damon! What is wrong with you? I was going to have to intervene, and that would earn *me* a trip to the Pit, alongside him, if this went any further south. *Shut the hell up.*

He ignored me, although he gave me a shove with his

magic. It pushed me away from the two of them. "She hasn't been right since you and Michael took her to the Lost City," he accused. "What did you do to her?"

"Your protectiveness is curious," Lucifer replied, "but unwarranted. If my brother and I had done anything to the vengeance demon, she would have told you. She is loyal to you, is she not?"

Damon flicked a glance at me, where I was pressed against the wall because of him. "She was. Her current loyalty leans toward angels these days." It came out in a snarl. His focused gaze bore into Lucifer. "You've brainwashed her, and I won't stand for it."

Lucifer's magic burst out of him, shoving Damon next to me and pinning him there. "Remember your place, archdemon," he snarled back.

I'd only witnessed snippets of Damon's magic here and there through the years. The full force of his calling it up created a fresh tremor in the dungeons, causing the ground beneath my feet to crack and the walls to shake. Debris from the ceiling rained down on me, and Cole shouted an expletive right before Damon broke through Lucifer's hold and launched himself at the archangel.

Herculean forces slammed into each other. Lucifer's wings became visible as he blocked the attack and sent Damon crashing into the far wall. Damon rebounded and tackled Lucifer to the ground.

I tried to shout, but my vocal cords were frozen. I desperately wanted to get to Rad and protect him, but I couldn't move. Even though I'd broken through Damon's grip on me earlier, what held me in place now wasn't his.

Lucifer's mojo not only kept me from moving, it formed a protective bubble around Rad. The sliver of Lilith's magic continued to hang in the air, undisturbed.

The angel and demon traded blow after blow, their magic and fists doing a number on each other. I yanked at my magical chains, wishing one of them would knock into me on the off chance it might break me loose. They didn't.

Kirill appeared in the corridor outside the cell, and Cole held him back, the two of them spectators. Kirill watched in shock, while Cole seemed to analyze each fighter's ability and cunning. I mentally tried to get them to step in and do something, but my telepathic abilities did not work with either demon. While Cole could often read my mind, it was only because we had worked together for so long and knew each other so well. He no doubt knew what I was thinking at that moment, but was enjoying the show too much to take action.

My frustration and anger upset my inner demon. I drew as much magic as I could from the quaking ground under me and fed her with it.

She gobbled up the Earth energy and sucked the frenzied magic all around her into my system. I prodded her to break through my restraints, but even with the extra power, she could not free me.

Which really pissed me off.

Rage ripped through me, and the wave of it at least allowed me to grit my teeth and tense my muscles. I fought against my restraints, pushing her to crack any and all magic that wasn't mine from controlling me.

Something deep inside me broke open, a vast well. The

force of it, as it rushed to the surface, made me gasp, the bubble dissolving as if I'd spilled acid on it.

In the next breath, I was moving, throwing myself between the two and yelling. "I command you to stop this instant!"

My voice reverberated in the space like a timpani drum. Angel and demon jerked away from each other, puppets on strings. They stood frozen, staring at me in shock, gasping as blood ran from various injuries on their faces and throats. Their knuckles were split open, their clothes torn and in disarray.

I vibrated with power, waves of it pouring off of me. It was my turn to pin each of them against a wall, and from their expressions, neither could grasp that I had the ability to do so.

My demon was heady with the power, and I knew she'd fully surfaced. Lucifer's surprise bordered more on curiosity, but Damon was familiar with her. He'd seen me lose control more than once, but I'd never been able to match him in the power department.

"Now," I said, my voice sounding more like myself. Inside, I was teetering on the edge of that deep, vast well of darkness that was feeding my magic. It was beyond anything I understood, and I feared it was part of the Omni nucleus I had ingested. "This ends." I glared at Damon. "You're right. I'm different, but it's not his fault." I switched my glare to Lucifer. "I apologize for his attack. It won't happen again, especially over me. I want your promise that you will not send him to Hell over this. We need him here."

Damon was affronted that I was making an apology on his behalf and insinuating he couldn't handle this himself. I didn't care. Lucifer looked as though he was going to be belligerent about it all, but seeing as I had shocked him and still held him captive, even against the fresh onslaught of magic he was hitting me with, he seemed to reconsider.

He spoke to Damon. "What you sense is Kali's divine essence making an appearance."

Damon opened his mouth to argue, then snapped it shut. He looked me over. "Her what?"

"Her angelic nature," Lucifer said. "Have you not sensed it?"

Cole snickered, and everyone glanced his way. None of us was smiling. This was no joke, and his amusement died. "No shit?" he asked. "Kali, an angel?"

Great. Now *that* secret was out. My demon wanted to claw out someone's eyes, but there was no good candidate. I soothed her, petting Volante, and internally stepping away from that bottomless nexus of power.

She didn't go quietly, but I managed to shove her back into her cage. I was going to need to fight someone to truly satiate her. "It's just the *vitium* in me," I said, hoping Damon, Cole, and Kirill would believe it. It's what I'd been telling myself in response to those pesky nudges insisting it was something else.

Damon glanced at Lucifer. Lucifer wouldn't meet his eyes. So much for his help. "You're lying," Damon said to me.

"I don't know for sure what it is," I admitted. "I've been hanging around fallen angels too much, and then Michael stuffed some of his mojo inside me. It's still there, I think. That's all it is."

I released my chokehold on them, and they staggered from the absence of it.

"How did you do that?" Lucifer asked, perplexed.

"I'm not entirely sure." It wasn't a lie. I had an idea of where it came from, but not how I'd activated it. It seemed to trip when I became enraged, but this day so far had been out of my control, and maybe that had as much to do with it as anything. I hate when I'm not in control.

Kirill stepped into the cell, holding out the jar. He seemed totally flustered and a bit wary of me. "This should contain it."

We all glanced at the sliver still hanging above Rad. With everyone's attention on it, it seemed to once more be sentient, turning to look at each of us. Lucifer took the jar and captured it inside.

"Can I have it?" I asked.

He wiped blood from under his nose with the back of his hand. "For what?"

A plan was forming in my mind. It wasn't complete yet, but I had several ideas on how to reverse-engineer this string of magic to end Lilith's terrorizing reign in Chicago. "It's time to give Lilith a dose of her own magic."

Rad startled us, sucking in a loud breath, sitting straight up, and looking around wildly. He took in Damon and Lucifer's appearance, the cracked floor and walls, and then his gaze landed on me. His smile suggested I was the best thing he'd ever seen. "What happened?"

I dropped to my knees beside him and hugged him. "You're going to be just fine, Chaos demon."

He hugged me back. "Good to know. Can we get out of here?"

I glanced at Lucifer. "I have your word, right?"

He didn't so much as glance at Damon, but I could feel his irritation. "I won't send him to the Pit. For now," he added.

Damon snarled.

Lucifer snarled back.

I rolled my eyes.

CHAPTER TEN

When I decided to take Rad to my place, the archdemon and archangel were suddenly allies again.

"The Chaos demon should remain under surveillance and in quarantine," Lucifer said, "until we are sure of his recovery."

"Since this cell is destroyed," Damon added, "I'll secure another for him."

Rad scowled. "I'm fine."

The fact that he wasn't vomiting and that he was upright told me he was on the mend. It didn't solve the fact that he had little black Omni voids swimming around in his spinal fluid, but I'd take a victory lap that we'd stopped Lilith's influence.

"I can handle him." I pointed at the jar. "Once I have a firm plan, I'll be back for that."

I led Rad over the piles of rusted metal particles. "What happened to the bars?" he asked.

"I'll tell you on the way to my place." I met Cole's frown. "I'm going hunting later. Want to come?"

"What about the heart in your desk drawer?" he asked. "Shouldn't we look into that now?"

"Heart?" Damon, Kirill, and Lucifer all said in unison.

Cole traced a thumb over one of his throwing knives. "Seems someone wanted Kali's attention, but we have no clue who or why."

"You didn't think to mention this earlier?" Damon barked.

I quirked a brow. "When, exactly? I was a bit busy, trying to save Rad and all." At his burning glare, I reined in my patience. "I need to tackle one dragon at a time. The heart is another of Lilith's ploys. I'll handle it later."

Maddy, who'd been hanging back, offered a different idea. "Or a vampire's." When we all looked at her, she shrugged. "Classic calling card."

I hadn't known that. You learn something new every day, even when you've been alive as long as I have.

Rad sagged against the wall. "We should look into it."

He was in no condition to do more than take a nap. "Cole, Maddy, and I will do that. You're going to work on getting your strength back."

When he didn't argue, I knew I was right. He needed red meat, eight hours of shut-eye, and possibly some rejuvenating sex. In that order.

And I'd be happy to play nursemaid.

Kirill pushed past me with the container. "He should remain in the infirmary so I can watch him."

"Not gonna happen, pops," Rad said.

Which pissed off the Pestilence demon. Kirill made a

sour face and shook his head. "I don't know why I even try to help you two."

Cole glanced at Damon. "Can you spare me for the rest of the day?"

Damon said nothing for a long, tense moment. His dark eyes bore into me as he finally answered. "Keep an eye on her."

Cole nodded. "Roger that."

Cole ordered Maddy to accompany him to the garage. They disappeared, and I forced Rad to put an arm around my shoulders to help him up the stone steps.

Damon followed. When we reached the ground floor, he disappeared. I left Rad at the reception area, where Neve usually manned the desk and Lainie, our house mother, had her own private cubicle. Neither was present.

I caught Lucifer on his way to the elevator. "How did you know?"

He knew what I was referring to. "It's obvious."

"It is?"

"Have you not known all along?"

I shook my head. "I wish I'd never found out."

"Is it so repugnant to you to carry angelic power?"

"I'm a demon. Of course it is."

"You're a unique hybrid. You should embrace it."

"Not sure I want to," I admitted. "Even if I did, I don't know how."

"Hmm." A noncommittal response. Then, "I will train you. Like the Fallen, you require careful handling."

Oh, hell no. "No offense, but I'll pass."

The corner of his mouth twitched. Not a smirk. Not a frown. "You'll regret that decision, but it's yours to make."

He walked away, smug and arrogant as always.

Little did he know I had a plan he'd hate. But I needed to take control of this situation.

Rad refused my assistance as we headed to the parking garage. He was silent, either because of his exhaustion after being possessed or because he was giving me the cold shoulder over the angel thing. He'd told me before that I glowed during sex. There were other signs, too, that I'd ignored.

But I had too much on my mind to make idle conversation or get drawn into an argument with him, so I stayed silent, too. Only our footsteps on the concrete stairs accompanied us.

Avoiding an argument was a moot point when we arrived to find Cole and Maddy waiting outside the Land Rover for us. They both had expressions that told me we weren't going anywhere until I explained.

"We can talk on the way to my place," I told them.

I opened the door to the backseat to hustle Rad inside, but he crossed his arms and leaned on the SUV next to Maddy. "Talk now," he said.

Oh goody. An ambush.

"There isn't much to say, and it doesn't change anything. I'm still me. I don't believe there is true angel essence in my veins. It's a side effect of Michael's sword and what he shared with me. It's activated my vitium divinity, that's all."

None of them seemed to buy it.

"It changes everything," Cole said.

I itched to avoid this conversation in the worst way. "Like what? I am who I am. I'm still a vengeance demon, and I have done, and will continue to do, everything I can to protect those I care about. I have no love for angels, and you all know that. I certainly don't plan to embrace anything that has to do with them."

I yanked the keys off the pegboard and climbed into the driver's seat. "In or out?" I called to the three of them.

Maddy and Rad climbed into the backseat. Cole came around to my side and held out his hand. "I drive."

Back to normal. Good. "Only if you're not going to be a crabby baby about this."

He grabbed me by the arm and hauled me out of the seat. "For your insolence, I get to pick the music."

I hid my sigh of relief that he hadn't stuck a knife in me just to see if I would glow. "That's asking a lot, since your taste in music is atrocious. Maybe I should walk."

He acted like he was going to cuff me upside the head, but he smiled and purposely missed as I ducked. I went around to the passenger seat and climbed in. A minute later, we were hitting the freeway.

"How long have you known?" Maddy asked.

Damn. The conversation wasn't over. "Not long. I honestly thought it was part of my *vitium* status. I don't feel any different." That wasn't exactly true, but it was because of the Omni essence, not the angel mojo. I sent multiple texts, asking the recipients to meet us at my house. "Angel power still makes me itch. I hate it. If I were truly one of them, why would that happen?"

No one had an answer.

We stopped at a fast-food place to grab breakfast sandwiches, hash browns, and coffee. We ate on the way, and I was grateful for the silence. I had some big explaining to do, but I wanted them all together, and I needed to give them an out if they decided what I told them was too much for them to handle.

Before we entered my home, I placed my hand on the stones outside the door. I called up Earth energy and sent my magic on a scouting expedition inside, searching for any signs she was paying me a visit. I sent a second wave to look for booby traps or any other surprises she might have left.

I found none, but there were two entities waiting for us. Voices and singing came from my office.

While the others shed their jackets and grabbed drinks from the kitchen, I made my way to see who was occupying my chair. I found Sal seated at the desk and Shayne lounging on the sofa across from it with a magazine in hand. My laptop was open, and a video of a bunch of singing and dancing teens played while Sal bopped along to the music via my earbuds. He used chopsticks to slurp up noodles from a white takeout box.

Shayne, another of our *vitium* group, glanced at me, running a hand through his shaggy blond hair. "Took you long enough, mate." He removed his dirty boots from the corner of the desk and straightened. "The gang all here?"

I snapped the lid of the computer shut, and Sal jerked back, removing one of the earbuds. "Hey! That's my favorite K-pop video."

I rolled my eyes. "Join us in the living room."

When the others saw Sal, they went on alert. Rad was lying back on my sectional and sat upright. Maddy had been rocking in my recliner, and she stopped and bared her fangs. Cole took two steps toward the priest, hand on the dagger hilt at his waist.

I held up a hand. "Sal and Shayne are here at my request."

Di and JR burst through the front door. "Got here as fast as traffic would allow," Di said, shucking off her violently pink wool driving coat and checking her hair. "Did we miss anything?"

"We haven't started yet," I told her. "Grab a drink if you want one."

"I could use coffee." She tossed her coat on the pile near the door. "Want anything, JR?"

He shook his head, nervous to see the gathered crowd. He had a gaming headset around his neck and carried his own laptop. While he was an expert at all things related to technology, people weren't his thing. He didn't meet any of our eyes and hurried over to a spot in the farthest corner from us, where he plunked down and immediately opened the computer.

Now, all we needed was Dru.

"What's going on?" Rad asked. He was wan with smudges darkening the skin under his eyes.

"I'll explain in a minute."

Cole used his dagger to point at Sal. "That was all a ruse back at the Institute?"

Sal sucked in a noodle. He'd brought the box with him. "It's been a ruse for months, but none of you caught on, thanks to my superior acting skills."

"Not exactly true," I added hastily at the disbelieving looks from my friends. "Sal and I are working together for a common cause, not because we like each other."

He blew me a fake kiss.

His change in behavior was quite surprising to everyone.

The solemn priest in his drab robes was gone, replaced by a guy in jeans and a T-shirt with an attitude.

Shayne chuckled. "The act was solid, mates. You even had me fooled until today."

The security system alerted me to the fact that someone else was about to join us. The way my blood warmed at the approach of the master vampire alerted me as well. "Come in, Dru," I called, barely raising my voice above normal. His superior hearing would pick up on it.

He entered, shuffling into the living room, his dark eyes surveying the group. His more formal attire consisted of a smoky gray suit, a satin shirt two shades lighter, and a matching tie. "My Queen." He dipped his head. "And here I thought we were having a *private* meeting."

Seduction oozed from his tone. Rad bristled. Maddy grinned.

"Glad you made it." I winked. "I'm in need of your services."

I gestured for him to take a seat, but he stayed standing, watching me carefully. "In regard to what we spoke of yesterday?"

I nodded. "Can I get you a glass of blood?"

His eyes smoldered. "Only if it's yours."

More bristling and grinning, along with nervous coughing. "Not today, I'm afraid."

"I could really do with some sleep," Rad growled. "What is this all about?"

I'd wanted this meeting because I was tired of carrying this burden on my own, but now that they were all here, looking at me, I felt nervous about what I was about to propose. "I want to share information with you that cannot leave this room or be discussed with anyone outside of it. Knowledge of this will put you in extreme danger. All of us have gone up against some very nasty entities in the past, but what I'm about to tell you makes all of that seem like child's play. This is your one chance to bow out before it goes any further. I'm going to ask you to go on a perilous mission with me that has no room for error. None."

 I took a breath and met each person's eyes. "Imagine your worst nightmare and then escalate it a thousand times. This battle will most likely leave me and anyone who joins me at the mercy of forces like none we've ever faced before. I cannot emphasize strongly enough the hazards involved. Therefore, I'm giving you an out. If you're smart, you'll take it. Get up, grab your coat, and leave. No shame, no judgment, no contempt. I can't protect you from the hazards of this mission, and bailing now is the smart thing to do."

Everyone stayed seated, continuing to stare at me. Their energies were all over the place with a mix of confusion, curiosity, and...excitement. *Weirdos.*

"Let me stress this again," I continued. "If you stay, you're agreeing to my rules and stipulations. There is no margin for error, and I won't tolerate insubordination. If you defy me, you'll be removed from the mission and may possibly end up imprisoned in a dimension devoid of everything."

That got their attention. "I'm afraid I need more information before I can make a decision regarding this," Dru said.

"Same," Di added. "Although it does sound rather thrilling."

JR was up and sliding toward the door. That was no

surprise. While he was a loyal employee, he was human, and I hadn't really expected him to eagerly join my ragtag bunch. Still, it was disappointing. I needed his skills.

Di noticed the tech nerd trying to escape and jumped up to block his way. "Where do you think you're going?"

He froze, eyes darting around the room to land on inanimate objects rather than any of us. "She said we could leave if we weren't on board with this."

"You're one of us," Di said. "And Kali invited you here because you must be important to this mission." She glanced at me. "Right?"

"I'm not like you," JR said under his breath. "You're all... superheroes, or whatever. I'm just me."

"We've talked about this." She laid a friendly hand on his shoulder. "You don't give yourself enough credit."

"It's okay." I moved toward the two of them. "You're free to go, JR. No hard feelings."

Di gave a huff. "If something happens to Kali, you won't have a job."

JR flicked his gaze to me. Away. He hugged his laptop. "I'm no hero."

I smiled. "You're a brilliant mastermind when it comes to manipulating computer systems and finding information that none of us can."

"Yeah, so?"

"What if I offered you the multiverse version of the internet?"

He pushed his glasses up his nose and met my eyes again. This time, his gaze held. "What do you mean?"

"The quantum field. Talked about and conceptualized by the great minds of our time but never actually accessed to any relevant degree. I can hook you up with it. Total access."

His eyes bugged out as he realized what I was offering. "How?"

I swept my hand toward his previous seat. "You have to stay and agree to my terms in order to find out."

Was it manipulation? Dangling a carrot he couldn't refuse? Yes. Yes, it was. I needed him.

Still hugging the computer, he turned and went back to the chair, slumping down and staring at the floor. Not to avoid our eyes, but in a state of wonder.

I addressed the rest of the group. "Anyone else? I won't try to make you stay, but just like JR, I've chosen each of you for a specific reason."

No one left. They glanced at each other, full of silent questions, but also a brand of loyalty that could not be bought or severed.

I gave everyone another minute, getting a cup of coffee for myself in the kitchen before I returned.

I still had a full house. "Good. Let's get down to business."

CHAPTER ELEVEN

I stood near the fireplace in the sunken living room, looking at each member of my group. I wanted them to understand the gravity of the situation, yet I worried I wasn't emphasizing enough just how dangerous it was.

"It's not easy for me to ask for help," I admitted. "But this isn't something I can do alone. I want to, but I can't."

Rad sat forward, elbows on his knees. The tiredness still exuded from his body, but he was now alert in a different way than before. But he already knew about the Omnis and hadn't run yet. "I'm not going anywhere. I'm all in."

Several others murmured and nodded. I sipped my coffee, wondering how to present this without overwhelming them. Unfortunately, there wasn't any way to do that. "You're all familiar with the entity that humans refer to as God." At their nods, I went on. "That entity is one of several called Omnis. I met one of them recently, and it's not an experience I think of fondly. After that meeting, I became aware of information that very few supernaturals have ever heard of, and for good reason."

I gave them the briefest version possible of what the Omnis were and what they were after. "The one we call God is a creator. The other three are destroyers. And they don't just destroy, they obliterate. They want to obliterate us. To completely annihilate this world, this universe, this dimension. If they succeed, there won't be anything left. Not a trace of any of us."

A variety of reactions emerged—brow lifts, wide eyes, covert shuffles. No one spoke.

I toyed with the cup. "Before I go any farther, you must know that at least one of them walks the Earth. Not God, but one of his enemies. One of the others who wishes to bring about our annihilation. That entity has chosen a physical body and walks among us. It may be able to access your mind and memories, and so after I share this with you, I'll need to erect a barrier around this information—and your ability to share it."

Maddy sullenly crossed her arms, sinking deeper into the cushions of the sofa. "How do you do that? You're not a witch, and if this being is so powerful, won't it just break through anything you can put up?"

"We're going to find out." I finished off the coffee. I was going to need a lot more, or maybe something stronger. "When I met one, I sort of...tore off a chunk of it and absorbed it."

Reactions escalated over that. Most of them reeled back, realizing what that meant. I'd always been abnormal in their eyes, but this made me a full-fledged freak of epic proportions. Worse than being an angel.

"So...you're one of *them* now?" Di asked.

"Puts a few things in perspective, doesn't it?" I paced in front of the fireplace. "I don't feel any different, and believe me, I have no urge to obliterate anything." Well, that wasn't exactly true, but it was best that I kept that to myself.

"The way you dissolved the bars of my cell," Rad said, "was accessing that power."

"And how you commanded Lucifer and Damon to stop fighting," Cole said. "And they did. You locked them in place."

Dru smirked. "I'm sorry I missed that."

"It was epic," Maddy said with a grin. "The look on their faces was priceless."

This wasn't funny, yet considering the gravity of what I was telling them, I was glad for it. I could still feel that nexus of power deep inside me, itching to break free.

"The power I ingested should give me the ability to protect your minds from the Omnis who seek to learn our plans. Initially, I intended for all of us to go about our daily routines so as not to alert them, especially the one I'm ninety-nine percent sure is keeping a close eye on me. Grooming me to find what it needs."

"And what does this being need?" Dru asked.

"God stole an important piece from each of his siblings, turned them into artifacts, and hid them here on Earth. They need those pieces returned in order for them to be at full power."

Rad kicked back, crossing his ankles. "We have to find the artifacts."

"Where are they?" Maddy asked.

Sal set down the now-empty box and pulled a folded

parchment from his back pocket. "Good question, young vampire. That's the problem. We don't know."

Dru stood stock-still except for the knuckle he ran over his chin. "What are they?"

"Another good question." I paused my pacing. "We don't know that either."

Di gave an exasperated chuckle. "How are we supposed to find them, then?"

"Sal and I have been narrowing down possibilities. Ruling out what they can't be. I think I have an idea of what all three of them are and where they're located. The thing is, I need to divide up the information. It's safer for you and for me if none of you has the complete picture. Since I have some of the Omni essence inside of me, I'm able to restrict what the others might pick up on, but even if I put a barrier around your thoughts, it's still possible they could find a way to infiltrate them and sabotage what I'm doing."

I glanced out the window and back at my audience. "Do you understand? We are dealing with an untested and unknown set of possibilities. I have to outthink entities that I've never encountered before and have no guidebook to tell me what will work and what won't. There's no precedent for what we're doing. Giving you even this much information endangers you, but I know I can't do this on my own. That's why I've brought you in. I still want to protect you as much as possible."

"Just tell us what you need us to do," Cole said.

I could always count on him to cut through the extraneous to get to the bottom line. "As with any wartime strategy, I'm going to do some scouting. Test a few theories and see what emerges. I want to pair up each of you with a

partner and give you an assignment. You'll report your find-
ings to me, and only me. I'll take each of these pieces and put
them together into the big picture, and we'll proceed from
there."

I felt a new presence outside the front door. Before she
could knock, I called, "We're in the living room."

Faron, the Fate, and her bodyguard, Bane, sauntered in.
She was dressed in leather from head to toe, and he wore
cargo pants, military boots, and a jacket with so many
pockets it could hold a small arsenal. "Got your message,"
Faron said. Both of them took in the gathered group before
they exchanged a look. "This isn't some kind of intervention,
is it?"

They'd already met everyone, so introductions weren't
necessary. "I need your help predicting the future," I said.

"You know I can't do that, right?" She hooked her
thumbs in her belt loops. "Based on your intentions, I might
be able to tell you what outcome to expect, but as soon as you
make a different decision, that changes."

I was well aware of how her gift worked, and while I
would probably make many decisions in the coming weeks
that would alter outcomes, I needed to know whether my
current plan was viable and whether it would get anyone I
cared for killed. "You're here to read my current intentions
and tell me two things: do I have a chance at succeeding at
what I'm attempting, and will it cost me the lives of any of
the people in this room?"

She narrowed her eyes. "Sounds ominous."

"What you're about to become privileged to puts you
and him in danger." I jutted my chin toward Bane. "But your

insight can make the difference between saving this entire universe and having it obliterated."

Her brows jacked up. "What have you gotten yourself into this time?"

"If you want to know, then you'd better start looking at my fate threads."

She glanced at Bane again, as if considering whether she was willing to put his life on the line.

Interesting. They didn't seem to be romantically involved, yet there was a connection between them that couldn't be denied. It went deeper than physical attraction, and they tried to hide it behind sarcasm, sniping at each other, and acting as though they were forced to be partners rather than choosing it.

He gave her a subtle nod, letting her know that he was in if she was. She took a couple of breaths, deciding, and then stepped toward me. "Let down your guard."

Easier said than done. Even before I knew about the Omnis, I kept my thoughts sheltered from the world. It was ugly inside my head, and the idea of anyone invading my thoughts and memories had long ago scared me. I hated sharing anything on a good day, much less my private chaos on the bad ones.

I mimicked her, dragging in several deep breaths and letting them out slowly. I closed my eyes and imagined opening up the shields I kept around my thoughts and intentions. She gave me time and space to get comfortable with the idea—at least as comfortable as I could be—before she sent a gentle probe into my mind.

Gentle, but yet unwanted, and my shields immediately snapped into place. My eyes flew open, and my demon growled. Faron physically jerked back, recoiling with her magic, and Bane was instantly by her side, his hand on his blade at his waist.

In unison, Rad, Cole, and Dru surrounded me. Di and Maddy shoved their way between me and the Fate.

Sal, Shayne, and JR sat transfixed, watching the show with their undivided attention, but only JR seemed concerned.

I waved everyone off. "It's okay. My fault. This isn't something I'm comfortable with, but it's necessary all the same. Everybody, sit down and relax."

Faron murmured something to Bane, and while the others reluctantly backed away, he strode to the bottom of my staircase and planted his feet.

The Fate held up placating hands. "I thought you were ready. I didn't mean to push you too quickly."

I rolled my shoulders and cracked my neck. "I thought I was ready, too. Let's try again."

This time, not only did I lower my shields, but I created a pathway into my thoughts, beckoning her magic to me. This seemed to work better, my demon believing the intentional invitation was so I could trap her. I smothered that idea as quickly as it rose, feeling the barbed tickle of Faron's power tugging at my thoughts.

With all my willpower, I focused on my plan to find the artifacts and incapacitate the Omnis. As she absorbed the information about the powerful entities and what I intended to do, her shock was a palpable punch, repulsed by the knowledge I was handing her. Out of all of them, she understood the true consequences hanging in the balance of every decision I made from this point forward.

Her power was an unusual one. The magic that gave her the ability to bind the threads of fate and bring about the inevitable end of all things, twinned with the calculating essence inside of me that I had yet to completely grasp or figure out how to manage. It liked her power, stroking it and trying to draw more into its well of unlimited potential.

At least no one, not even Damon, could read her mind. She was also used to consuming an overwhelming amount of information and potential choices. I thought she would handle it.

She swayed on her feet, her eyes closing, and a blissful look came over her face. Bane didn't move, but shifted to a heightened state of attention. Could he feel what she was feeling?

My demon both feared and craved the Omnis' power. The few tastes I'd had so far had been like teasers. Being connected to Faron and drawing on her power, the void inside me sprang open like a bear trap.

I gasped, and so did she.

Something wasn't right. She wasn't only reading my mind and seeing the future my decisions would create—she was in *The Unknowing*.

Before I could tell her to stop, the bear trap snapped shut.

CHAPTER TWELVE

"Stop," I screamed, but it came out as a whisper. I tried again, pushing against the connection mentally. "*Stop!*"

Rad was by my side in a heartbeat. Bane by Faron's. They jerked us apart, but it wasn't physical space that would cut the cord.

"What's happening?" Rad yelled.

"You're hurting her," Bane accused.

I had to tune them out. Diving into the void, I latched onto a silvery thread. It was Faron's fate power, sparkling in the darkness. Using my inner demon and some angelic mojo, I drew it to me and wound it into a ball. Then I yanked for all I was worth.

In the back of my mind, I felt her yank back. She wasn't cooperating; the call of The Unknowing was too strong to resist.

Dammit, Faron! I sent wave after wave of power down the thread. Rad, Bane, and the others shouted and jostled us, tugging us farther and farther apart, even as I was coiling my power around hers to bring her to me.

My demon roared with feral hunger, snapping her teeth at the void. The bottomless pit I'd touched earlier awakened and flooded me with a raw force.

I punched Faron with it. *Wake the hell up!*

In a flash of silver light, the thread exploded.

I slumped to the floor, caught by Rad's strong hands. Blinking, I saw Faron had also collapsed.

"What did you do to her?" Bane snarled.

I couldn't make my mouth work. Thought was absent, still stuck in The Unknowing's after effects. It was similar to a hangover—my limbs and brain were numb.

Rad sat me on the edge of the sofa. "Kali, look at me."

I focused on his face. The chiseled jaw, his beautiful eyes. He hadn't shaved in the past twenty-four hours, and whiskers covered his cheeks and chin. The lines around his eyes seemed more pronounced, his lips fuller. I noticed each and every hair on his head, the way his earlobes connected to his neck, his sleek, straight nose...

"Kali!" He shook me slightly. "Are you all right?"

My demon growled her displeasure at being severed from Faron and the Omni's power, but she was willing to be distracted by him. My voice came out raspy. "Yes," I said, although I was far from it. "Faron...is she...?"

Bane had laid her down on the opposite end of the sofa. She sat up groggily, rubbing her forehead. "What in the fates?" She sounded as out of it as I was. "What just happened?"

Bane seethed at me. "I should kill you."

"Try it." Cole stepped in front of me like a shield. "It will be the last thing you do."

Bane bared his teeth.

I touched Cole's lower back. "It's okay. Everybody take a breath."

Cole reluctantly moved aside. Rad rubbed my arm. Faron and I stared at each other across the cushions.

"We need to talk," she said. "Alone."

Bane shook his head. "Not gonna happen. Whatever's going on, you tell all of us."

She gripped his hand. "It has to do with her fate."

My stomach dropped. Bane swore under his breath. If she wasn't willing to share with the group, it had to be bad.

Rising on shaky legs, I motioned her toward my office. Rad's chaos magic swam around me, but I gave him a smile and a wink, trying to act like I was unconcerned with whatever she was going to lay on me.

As soon as I shut the door, she whipped around. "You can't save us."

My temples pounded. I slid into my chair and rubbed them. "I have to try."

She shook her head. "Doesn't matter what you do. That...*thing*...inside you? It's going to devour everything."

"You saw its fate rather than mine, didn't you?"

A sharp nod, her eyes full of fear. She swallowed visibly. "It wants to eat us. All of us. This entire universe." Her voice dropped. "And it's going to succeed."

Her power was impressive, but it did have limits. "You just reminded me before we did this that you can't predict the future, only a version of what might happen based on the present moment."

She slammed her hands on the desk. "This is different. I saw it all. Every scenario that could play out, no matter what decisions you make. They all end in our complete oblivion. Nonexistence. Extinction." She shuddered and straightened, rubbing her arms as if chilled. "I've never experienced anything like it. What's worse, I wanted to give in. Let it take me. It was so...peaceful."

"The first time I encountered it, I felt the same way."

"If you hadn't ripped me out of there, I would be gone right now. I'm already a forgotten, arcane relic, but this..." Another shudder. "It would be like I'd never existed."

"That's what the Omnis want—to wipe out everything. All of them except God. I can't let that happen."

She snorted. "You can't stop it."

"I think I can. If God has thwarted them this long by keeping the artifacts hidden, what I need to know is this: will tracking the locations of those artifacts sabotage that? Should I leave well enough alone?"

One finger tapped her chin in thought. "Maybe."

"Not super helpful."

Plopping into the chair across from me, she kicked her feet up onto the edge of the desk and crossed her ankles. "Why are you hunting the artifacts?"

"Because a couple of archangels said that was the way to keep them safe, but I don't put too much stock in what angels tell me."

"Same. Why would they lie, though, if finding the artifacts will cause the destruction of everything, including them?"

"Been pondering that myself."

A knock came at the door. "Faron," Bane barked.

No question or further comment followed, just her name. She rolled her eyes. "Everything's fine. Be out in a minute."

I listened for his footsteps to retreat. It took a minute. His reluctance to leave her was evident in every step. "You've never told me where he came from or what exactly he is."

"It's not important."

"Everything is important right now. Details matter."

She chewed her bottom lip. "What I tell you doesn't leave this room."

I was amenable to that unless I discovered my theory was right. Odds were against it, but I needed to be sure. "How did you get tagged with him?"

"He comes from another dimension, one that's not talked about here. He's a god hunter." She waited for my reaction. I didn't give her one. "Not like in stories and songs by humans. The real thing. In the place he comes from, there are factions of gods and goddesses. They all seek ultimate power over each other, so they create their own hunters to kill their enemies. It's like a constant gang war."

In all my three-hundred-plus years, I hadn't heard of such a thing. "And he's one of their creations?"

"Imagine the Roman gods warring with the Greek gods. They all have similar origin stories and represent the same things, yet each believes they're superior. Their supernatural powers are fairly equal, so they need other ways to infiltrate and take out the opposition. That's where the god hunters come in."

"How did he end up here with you?"

"When my sisters abandoned me, that's the dimension they went to. They sent him back to protect me. There are entities and coteries here that wish to trap me and use me to manipulate the future. My sisters want him to protect me, and if I were to get caught by one of those entities, his orders are to eliminate me."

I rocked in my chair, considering that. She'd just put a new light on things, and I flipped through my options of how to use it to my advantage. "He has the power to do that?"

"I hope to never find out, but I believe so."

"You've been in contact with your sisters? You're sure they sent him?"

"We haven't spoken in person, but the three of us had a codeword that we made up. We're the only ones who know it. When he arrived, he delivered their message with that codeword. I had no reason to doubt him."

She wasn't gullible and had been around far longer than I had. Yet, I had plenty of reasons to doubt her guardian's intentions. His origin story deserved more investigation, too. "You touched the power of the Omni. It's called The Unknowing. Have you ever experienced anything similar to that, especially around Bane?"

She jerked back like I'd slapped her. "You don't think...?"

"I have to pursue every angle. If he comes from a different dimension, and the only verification of his story is this codeword, it leaves a lot of room for interpretation. I can't eliminate him from my list of suspects, which means you're going to have to help me cross him off that list."

"I can't read his intentions."

Another strike against him. "And that doesn't concern you?"

"He doesn't have fate threads like the rest of us."

A new thought popped into my mind. "Does Aphrodite?"

"Yes. Even though she's a goddess, she has taken the form of a flesh-and-blood entity." Faron eyed me. "She's on your list, too?"

She hadn't been until that moment. The idea made me sick. "I can't rule out anyone until I can. Do you understand?"

Her feet hit the floor. She sat forward. "Who do you want me to start with since I can't read Bane?"

"Lucifer, Michael, and Damon. Out of all of us, except you, me, and Aphrodite, they are the most powerful. And if I put them head-to-head with the goddess, I'm still not sure she would win. The angels are the ones who told me about the Omni and explained what was going on. They're the ones who are sending me after the artifacts. I need to know they aren't manipulating the situation."

She pressed her hands against her thighs and stood. "I'm on it. I don't have many reasons to get close to them right now. Any chance you could facilitate that?"

I used a pen to doodle on my calendar. It was still stuck in November of the previous year. It had been a while since I'd looked at it. "I'll figure out something and be in touch. Meantime, I do have a couple more cases you could handle at the office if you're interested."

She headed for the door. "Mama's got to eat. I'll check in with JR."

"Send Bane in, would you?"

She stopped, her hand on the knob. "You want to talk to him alone?"

"Not particularly, but it's necessary."

"He won't like it."

"He doesn't like anything, does he?"

She chuckled. "Give him hell."

I was still smiling when his massive body trundled through the door and glared at me. "I'm not some ten-year-old you can call to the principal's office whenever you feel like it."

I motioned for him to close the door. "Have a seat."

He slammed it hard and crossed his arms. "I'll stand."

I shifted from my chair to the corner of the desk, not giving him the advantage of looming over me. "We have a situation on our hands, and I'd like to know which camp you're in."

He didn't so much as blink.

I continued. "Your powers are unusual, and I'm facing an unusual predicament. I'd like to see if you can help."

"My responsibility is to Faron."

"And she's in my camp. What I'm asking of you doesn't go against your oath to protect her. In fact, just the opposite."

"How so?"

I pulled out a ledger from the drawer. "This contains the names of all the innocents who've died because of me." I flipped the pages so he could see them. "If I don't stop what's coming, the entire world will be added to this book. Except the book won't survive, either. Neither will Faron."

That caught his attention, but he wasn't ready to give up his antagonistic attitude. "Drama queen, much?"

"I'm not overstating this. It's all true, and you can ask Faron to validate it. The entity I'm facing will obliterate all of us, possibly even you. At the very least, it will send you back to the dimension you came from, but your charge will not be coming with you. You can't save her unless you help me save all of us."

"Leading with the worst-case scenario in order to pull on my heartstrings?"

"Do you have heartstrings?"

That, at least, earned me a smirk. "If this place is going to go boom, I want to know how to get her out. Her sisters are in the other dimension; she can go there."

"Why would she want to? Doesn't sound like a great place to me. What good are Fates if they're surrounded by gods and goddesses? There is no fate loom there, is there?"

"You didn't answer my question."

"Faron knows what's coming. If she wants to escape to that realm, she can. Looks like she doesn't want to. Where does that leave you?"

He rocked back, considering. "This big bad entity...what is it?"

I filled him in. While his outward expression remained neutral, I saw the shock and fear, if only for Faron, warring inside him. "What do you think I can do?" he asked.

"She told me what you are. I need that kind of mindset to help me figure out how to defeat the Omnis. Especially the one we believe is walking around right under our noses."

He was silent for a long time. A new tug of war went on behind his eyes as he decided whether to help or not. "Let me think about it. This is a different kind of god than I'm used to. If it's all-knowing, all-sentient, I don't see how you can defeat it."

"On my own? I can't. But with you and the others? At least I have a fighting chance."

He took the book from my hands, his massive size

making my demon rear up and prepare to fight when he got close. He must've sensed it, his eyes locking on mine before he read through several of the entries. "Do you have heart-strings?"

I tipped my head toward the book. "I live every day with the burden of those innocent souls weighing on me. If I could change the past, I would."

He snapped the ledger shut and shoved it back into my hands. "If things go bad, I will remove her from this world before it's destroyed."

"Fair enough," I said, and then I told him what I needed him to do.

After he left, I brought each of the others in one at a time, giving them their assignments. They were all part of the whole, but I couldn't place the burden of carrying all of it on any single one of them.

It wasn't just for their own safety or mine. It was because knowing everything I was thinking and planning would be too overwhelming for them. They would lose focus because their minds would scatter to all the different possibilities. That was my job, to keep it all as organized and as systematic as I could.

When I exited my office, I found Rad asleep on the sectional. I didn't have the heart to give him his assignment, so instead, I woke him with kisses and took him upstairs. We showered, which led to other things, and then we fell into bed in an exhausted heap.

While I fought nightmares for a few hours, eventually I succumbed to a deep, dreamless sleep.

And in that oblivion, something watched.

CHAPTER THIRTEEN

I woke to the smell of espresso and warm pastries. Rad hovered over the nightstand, humming under his breath as he removed croissants and jelly donuts from a white bag before handing one of the small white espresso cups to me.

"Good morning, badass."

I pushed hair out of my face and struggled up on one elbow, admiring the fact he was naked from the waist up. His hair was tussled, and his formidable muscles made me lick my lips.

I blinked away the sleep and sipped at the warm liquid, releasing a sigh as it slid down my throat and warmed my chest.

The mattress dipped as he sat on the edge, tearing a piece off one of the croissants and feeding it to me. "Figured you needed sustenance."

"I hope you put a shirt on before you went to the bakery."

"Cami owed me a favor." He fed me a piece of a jelly

donut next. "She delivered. I made the espresso while I waited."

I licked at some filling stuck in the corner of my mouth. "Cami, huh?"

"She's a fan of my music."

The music he'd left behind for me. "I bet that's not all she was a fan of." I pointedly looked at his chest, licking my lips again for an entirely different reason.

He bent forward and kissed me, slipping his tongue into my mouth. He tasted of espresso and sugar, and I ran a hand behind his neck to keep him there long enough to remind him I was his number one fan.

In my heart, I knew it was unnecessary. We had a special bond, and although at one time I might have feared he would cheat on me, I no longer did. For one thing, he knew I'd cut off his balls if he did.

When we broke apart, his pupils were dilated, and his pulse had kicked up. Mine had as well. "I've been thinking about that," I said.

He took a bite of a croissant. "About what?"

"The chaos. The order. Your human side needs the creativity to keep the chaos from spinning out of control. That's why I brought the guitar to you when you were still in the dungeons. I was going to have you play me a song."

He took another bite and chewed thoughtfully. "I thought we decided Lilith caused the problem."

"She's part of it, but the reason she was able to possess you was because the chaos was riding the edge. You were keeping it controlled, but just barely."

He glanced down at his cup. "And here I thought I was doing a good job of it."

I ran my fingers down his forearm, feeling the muscles underneath my touch. "Why didn't you tell me you were struggling?"

He made a dismissive noise in the back of his throat. "You've been a little busy, Kali. You didn't need my problems on top of what you were already dealing with."

The room was dark except for the lamp casting a soft glow over our breakfast. I had no idea what time it was, never having invested in an alarm since my last one died. Usually, I used my phone, but it was nowhere in sight.

I gave his arm a slight squeeze. "You can always come to me, no matter what's going on. You are always my top priority."

His beautiful eyes met mine, but they were dark and mysterious in the dim light. "Like you come to me with everything?"

It was a sucker punch, and I felt it. My heart gave a little twinge. I wasn't good at sharing things, and he knew it, but he was right. Even when I felt I was doing the right thing to protect the others, he and I shared a bond that went beyond keeping secrets. "I'm sorry if I have to hold some things back in order to keep you safe. If I die, I need you to continue the fight."

"You're not going to die." He held out the last of the jelly donut. "Finish your breakfast first, Calina Dolce."

No one called me that anymore. I hadn't been that demon since I'd destroyed our mutual oppressor, Queen Maria.

But I understood why he used it, reminding me that he'd been with me in the beginning and was still with me, facing our potential end.

I let my lips linger on his fingers as I accepted the offering, slipping my tongue out to lick sugar from them. This was more than just food—it was a claiming.

We'd been separated for so long, and during that time, I had believed the worst of him. Now, I knew better. I knew of his deep, abiding devotion to me, and I wanted him to feel assured of mine to him.

I set our cups aside and climbed onto his lap. I ran my hands over his neck and shoulders, pressing my breasts against his chest and feeling him come to life under me.

Another claiming came next. He flipped me onto my back and undid the tie at his waist, letting the pajama pants fall to the floor. As he climbed onto the bed, he spread my legs wide, kissing me deeply. He took his time massaging my breasts and devouring my mouth. I sank my nails into his shoulders and arched under him, urging him on.

He trailed hot kisses down my neck and replaced his hand on my breast with his mouth. The other went between my legs and stroked me in a slow, maddening rhythm.

"I'm still hungry," he murmured against the skin of my stomach, making my muscles clench around the finger he slid inside me. He took his mouth to the sensitive cluster of nerves at my engorged folds.

I cried out, gripping his hair in a fist. The fingers that expertly played his guitars worked their magic on me. The lips that crooned love songs created a melody in my blood that made my heart sing.

The orgasm hit hard and fast, and I cried his name into the quiet of the room. My vision whited out, and I felt like my heart would explode.

In the aftermath, I gasped for air and blinked open my

eyes to find him staring down at me. "Still hungry?" I murmured.

He bit my lower lip. "Ravenous."

He lifted one of my legs over his shoulder and entered me in a single, swift motion. He was hard and thick, and I urged him deeper.

Had it only been a few hours since he'd taken me in the shower? It seemed as if days had passed, and I was just as hungry for him. For the reminder that we were still here, still alive, and not obliterated.

He drove himself into me relentlessly, burying himself so deep I cried out again.

The pain-laced sound brought him to a stop. He panted my name. "Kali?"

"It's okay," I whispered, stroking a lock of hair from his forehead. "Just give me a second."

"You're so tight," he said, the words strangled. "So, so tight. Like the first time we made love."

"That's because you're bigger."

His eyes cleared a bit, and the lust pushed back for a moment. "What?"

"Thicker, longer." I licked my lips. "Your chest is more muscular, too."

He glanced down at himself. "*Merde.*"

I chucked him under the chin. "*Giganto*," I teased in my native Italian. "*Straordinario.*" Exceptional.

"Am I going to...?"

"Morph? Let's hope not. I don't want to fuck myself." I pumped my hips, accepting him deeper again. "Just in case, hurry up."

He gave me a look that suggested this was no joking

matter, but since he was engorged to the point of no return, he accepted the kiss I laid on him and returned to his work.

The penetration was brutal and blissful. Something inside me shifted, and my demon liked it. All of it. Every single inch he plunged into me over and over until his body seized with his climax. As he called my name over and over, I tumbled into the sweetest of oblivions with him.

Not the oblivion of The Unknowing. No, this was the ultimate crescendo of our song. The earth literally moved, the stone walls of the church trembling in its wake. Dust fell from the ceiling. The windows groaned.

Time passed slowly as we both recovered. Rad shifted to lie beside me, staring into my eyes. "That was different," he said. "Earth shatteringly different."

I stroked a finger across his jaw and smiled, blissed out and not ready to speak yet. I traced his cheekbone and ran a finger over his eyebrow. I had no way of knowing if this was the last time I'd ever be able to do this.

Pushing the sad thought away, I placed a hand over his heart to feel its beating. My magic wrapped around him, soothing and grateful for his loyalty and devotion. "I love you."

He ran a hand up and down my arm and drew me into a kiss. "I love you. Nothing will ever change that."

What I was about to ask him to do might test that declaration. "I need to give you your assignment."

We sat up, pulling the sheets over us and leaning against the headboard. "I'm not going to like it, am I?"

There was no reason to lie. "No, but you have the most crucial part in my plan. You're the one who sees Damon on a daily basis. He talks to you. He'll be watching you, intent on discovering what's truly going on with me."

"What do you want me to do?"

I motioned for him to hand me my cup, and I sipped the now-cooled espresso. "First, I need to tell you everything I know. You're the only one I'm sharing this with, and you'll be at the most risk of betraying me."

He stiffened. "I would never."

"I know. Not intentionally, but if he's able to read your mind, you might not even realize he's done it."

"So why tell me everything? That doesn't make sense."

I intertwined my fingers with his. "Because I need you to know."

His gaze met mine. Understanding settled in that gaze. "Thank you for trusting me."

"You deserve to know everything. I don't want to keep any of this from you. If you decide it's too much and you want Dru to wipe your memories about it, I will totally understand and support that decision. But, you get the choice."

He squeezed my hand. "That means everything to me."

He already knew the basics, but I went into detail this time. About my encounter with the Omni and The Unknowing. What the archangels had explained, and my awareness to believe them, while still discerning the fact that at least some of it rang true. "Like I told everyone, I don't know what the artifacts are or where they're hidden, but I have a few ideas."

"Care to share?"

"If they're here on earth, they could be in the deepest part of the ocean. Under tons of sand. Inside a mountain so high, it has never been climbed or trapped in ice at one of the Earth's poles."

"Makes sense."

"Which would mean it also made sense to anyone, including the Omni I believe is hunting for them. It would have already scoured those places, able to go where we can't."

"Are you sure it's even in this dimension?"

I took another sip of my cold brew. "That's exactly what I'm wondering. God created Heaven and Hell, and we know that other dimensions exist. Some we've never heard about. But I also have to consider the fact that God covered the Earth with humans. He created a place where the environment undergoes extreme metamorphosis every few million years or so. Why? Why would he put the very creatures he created in danger?"

We discussed this for the next hour, trying to think like the one Omni we knew something about. We were still limited by that knowledge, but brainstorming together, we came up with a few different ideas that threw many of the conventions supported by the various religions out the window.

We both agreed that many of those could be a cover to mislead humans and others, like angels and demons, away from the truth. The more chaos He created, the less likely the Omni hunting the artifacts could weed through it.

"If we take the Garden of Eden origin story, and dissect it," I said, "we know several players who were there that might have valuable information for us."

He finished off the last of his espresso and set the cup aside. "Lucifer, for one. I assume Michael, as well. Amy?"

I nodded. "And Lilith."

His fingers stilled. "She was Adam's first wife."

"She refused to be dominated by him, so God sent her to Hell for it. What if that isn't the truth? What if she was the first to eat from the Tree of Knowledge of Good and Evil? What if the Tree is an artifact?"

He made a face. "But it doesn't exist anymore, and Eden was only ever a fairy tale."

Paradise—and maybe something else—lost. "The tree isn't mentioned in the Bible after Adam and Eve's expulsion, and most scholars believe it to be symbolic, but what if it's not? What if it and the Tree of Life were real? In my father's book, it states that the Tree of Life grants immortality. He wasn't the only one to mention that idea."

"Holy shit. Because it holds Omni essence."

"Exactly."

His head snapped sideways, his gaze locking with mine. "And now you have that essence."

I shrugged. Time to share the biggest of the truths I still needed to lay on him. "You do, too. I saw it in your spinal fluid."

He blinked, his mouth falling open. "How?"

"Because of me. Apparently, somehow I've infected you." He continued to bat his eyes and stare at me. I went on. "Lilith's possession aside, it's mutating your nature."

He swallowed hard and glanced down at his chest, then at me. "It's mutating both of us, isn't it?"

"My skills and abilities keep expanding. I'm not sure if it's due to that or the angel essence, but yes. It seems mostly likely that it's the Omni power." Apologies were hard for me.

I glanced down at my own cup. "I'm sorry I infected you with it."

He took the cup and set it aside, grabbing my hand. "You have nothing to apologize for. I've always told you that. I'm in this, no matter what happens. If you go down, I go with you."

"Damon needs to believe that you no longer feel that way. To get closer to him, you need to break up with me. It needs to be loud, dramatic, and in front of as many witnesses as we can get."

He reared back. "Break up with you? He'll never believe I'd do that."

"He will now that Lucifer outed me about being part angel. While I was upset he told everyone, I can use that to our advantage. The way you, Cole, and Maddy all reacted was perfect. Even Damon was shocked. And my lack of coming clean about it only emphasized the wedge it drove between all of us. You now have an excuse to break up with me. You no longer trust me. What demon would?"

He argued with me for a good ten minutes, and then I wrote out a script, hitting the highlights of our public breakup, and made him practice it with me. Maybe because he had been an entertainer for so many years and knew how to work a crowd, he was much better at following it than I was. I only hoped that when the showdown happened, I could be half as believable as he was.

Eventually, he made fresh espresso for us, and we showered again. When we were cleaned up and properly caffeinated, I stood in front of the fireplace, watching the script burn.

He came up behind me, a massive bulwark of contained

chaos, and wrapped his arms around me. "It's going to work. I hate it, but you're right. We can do this."

I leaned back into the comfort of his chest, picking up on his heartbeat. "Damon will be watching me, this house, and even my office. We can no longer meet here or at Sweet Investigations."

"Then where?"

"The second part of our breakup, I'm afraid. I'm going to publicly turn to Dru and embrace my role as Queen of the Chicago House. Maddy will be your point of contact. She will sneak you in and out of the House whenever you and I need to meet."

He turned me within the circle of his arms. "You can't be serious. You're going to let that vampire be your public rebound?"

"It makes sense. His ability with glamours can shield me somewhat from Damon. You, too, when we're together. The more I embrace my duties with the vamps, the less time I'll have to spend at the Institute. It's the best excuse I can come up with, along with hunting Lilith."

"Fine," he said through gritted teeth. "But I swear if he touches you..."

I squeezed his biceps. They were huge. "He's going to touch me, and he's going to kiss me in public in order to make you jealous and for Damon to believe our breakup is real. I have to do this, Rad. *We* have to do this. I hate it as much as you do."

He hugged me tightly and kissed the top of my head. "I do hate it. All of it. I thought once we stopped the prophecy about Azaria from coming true, things could go back to normal."

"Me, too."

His heartbeat thundered under my ear as I rested my head against his chest. "What about Lilith? Will she try to possess me again?"

"I'm still convinced she wants Damon because he's an Omni. Maybe she's one, too. Since we thwarted her last attempt at getting to his power, I doubt she'll try again right away. At least, not with you. I've added a block to your magic that will keep her out. Can you feel it?"

He mocked horror. "Without my consent?"

I shifted to stare up at him. "Yes."

He nipped at my lips. "Naughty demon."

I chuckled. "I'll do whatever I have to to keep you safe. It doesn't interfere with anything, only keeps out any magic that tries to hitchhike onto yours."

He sighed with resignation. "Does it ever end? This constant battle we're locked in?"

I was afraid it would—abruptly and catastrophically. "I don't know." I wrapped my arms around him and held him close. I thought of Faron's predictions. "I wish we had more time."

He held me close for long minutes, neither of us saying anything. We didn't need to. I sent up a prayer, doubting God was listening, but it was the only thing left to do.

CHAPTER FOURTEEN

Two days passed. As far as I knew, Rad was playing his part at the Institute, moping around, being short-tempered, and alluding to the fact that he and I were fighting.

I stared at the still-beating heart in my desk drawer, poking it with the end of a pen. Nothing happened. Waiting for whoever was on the other end of this calling card was taking more patience than I had.

Lilith still seemed like the most likely culprit, but Maddy insisted on doing some undercover work to see if any vampires in the area were disgruntled with me.

I had assured her there were plenty.

Faron and Bane sat on my couch, while Sophia ran through information regarding their next case. My office door flew open, and Vicky strode in, her normal state of pissed-offed-ness in full effect.

Her hair was growing out and refused to be tamed, chunks sticking up in all directions. "Why aren't you out there hunting her down?"

The heart skipped a beat. "I'm working on it. Do you have any leads?"

She smacked her hands on the top of my desk, leaning forward. Her eyes were wild with bloodlust. Actual blood-lust, since her vampire self was also riled up. Her pupils were red, her fangs on display. "I hired you to take care of her. To get revenge for me. You've done nothing."

At her entrance, Bane had assessed the threat and risen to his feet, keeping an eye on the two of us. He knew I could handle myself, and his concern was more for his charge than me, but I had sensed his loyalty stretching to include me to a certain extent since our talk.

I'd had a similar confrontation with Michael the previous day over the poltergeist incident. The archangel had been certain I'd purposely set him up to fail and had insinuated he would deposit me in the City of Lost Angels if I ever did such a thing again.

It just so happened that my companions had been present for that confrontation as well, and Bane had come to stand behind me, crossing his arms and doing his best imita-tion of a bodyguard.

Michael had been undaunted, but the incident had given Faron a chance to surf Michael's intentions and see if she could find anything suggesting he was misleading me about the Omni and the artifacts. She'd found nothing to support that theory.

We still needed to get her close to Lucifer, but that was tougher. He rarely left Amy and the baby, and I was staying as far from the Institute as possible.

I poked at the heart, drawing Vicky's attention to it. "Any guess as to who left this for me?"

She barely glanced at it. "Why would I care?"

"Because I believe it's from the very entity we're discussing. I just can't figure out what the message is. Any thoughts?"

Anything in connection with Lilith got her full attention. She approached the end of the desk to examine the heart more closely. Her nose crinkled, and she sniffed. "Witch magic. It reeks of it."

"Not demon or vampire?"

Her dark eyes snapped to me. "Vampire? You think I did this?"

I hadn't considered it, but she *was* both a witch and a vamp. I probably should have. "You weren't my first guess, no. Any clue as to who the witch might be?"

She leaned over and took a deeper inhale through her nose. When she straightened, a frown creased her forehead. "Smells like voodoo magic. Not my gig."

I rocked back in my chair. "Voodoo?"

Faron rose and skirted past Bane to join us. "Pissed off any African priests or priestesses lately?"

"No." This could be a way to get Faron close to Lucifer, though, and present an opportunity for me to put my breakup with Rad on full display. "But I know a vodun priestess who might be able to shed more insight."

Faron grasped my idea. "Keisha, Amy's friend."

I smiled. "An interesting paradox I find myself in and one that will work to our advantage."

"For what?" Vicky demanded. "How does that help you hunt down Lilith?"

A one-track mind, this one. "Want to come with us?" I

stood and considered my options for transporting the heart. "I could use your skills."

Her hair trembled with her anger. "You didn't answer my question."

"Guess you'll have to tag along and find out."

She huffed. "Fine."

I pointed to the heart. "How should we carry it?"

"I told you, voodoo isn't my jam."

"And yet, I bet you have the power to neutralize any magical residue on it."

Her ego was bigger than mine. She always had trouble refusing a challenge, especially when it called on her 'superior' talents. "Don't touch it directly. Wrap it in black cloth and place it inside a metal cooler. Bring salt."

Since I still didn't have a vehicle, I called Dru. A few minutes later, he arrived in his limo.

Ignoring the chauffeur, Maddy scrambled out of the back and held the door for him to exit. She made a face at Vicky, who snarled back. Dru strode to me, grasping my hand and kissing the top of it. "My Queen."

Vampire magic engulfed me. He wore a full suit, including a silk tie and pocket handkerchief. Over it, he'd thrown on a wool driving coat. His black hair soaked up the murky sunlight, and his eyes were pools of the darkest chocolate—slick, smooth, and oh-so-handsome.

And totally up for playing the role of my loving admirer who now welcomed a chance to seduce me.

I removed my hand. "Thanks for offering us a ride."

He motioned at the car. "What's mine is yours."

Vicky rolled her eyes. Maddy snickered. He shot both of them a look that squelched their rudeness and made the hair on my arms rise. Insubordination of any kind was not tolerated.

His power was juicy and ripe, teasing at mine, even though we were only acting out parts. I'd explained how I wanted him to perform, to help me sell my breakup with Rad, and he was all too happy to comply.

He positioned me next to him inside the limo's plush backseat, with Maddy on my other side, and our three companions across the aisle.

Maddy, too, was in on it. She lowered her voice as we drove through the streets of Chicago. "I heard what happened. Rad's an asshole."

I barely glanced at her, stiffening slightly as if her words had struck a nerve. "We'll work it out."

Dru huffed. "Why would you want to?"

The three across from us studied me intently. While Faron and Bane knew about my plan for learning who the Omni was, they weren't privy to all my machinations.

I fiddled with a string on my skirt. Despite the frigid temps, I'd worn it and my knee-high boots. Goosebumps pebbled the skin on my thighs even as the heater blasted us with warm air. "I've been in love with him since I was seventeen. He's my soulmate. He'll come around."

"No such thing," Vicky scoffed. "That's a stupid human falsehood that they tell themselves."

Faron glanced at Bane. He didn't return her look. *Hmm.* Did she consider him her soulmate?

I narrowed my eyes at Vicky. "You'll forgive me if I don't take advice from a washed-up witch who isn't even in a relationship, much less one that's existed for over three hundred years."

She clucked her tongue and stared at the passing scenery. "You're wasting your time on him."

While it wasn't part of the script, it played into our act perfectly. "You don't even know him."

"The former lead of the Chaos Demons?" She smirked. "Everyone knows Beaumont."

"You broke up?" Faron asked, eyeing me suspiciously.

I glanced away and took my time before answering. "He's upset about me being part angel."

Bane whistled under his breath. "Seems like a perk to me."

Faron elbowed him. "Why is he upset about that? It doesn't change who you are." She hesitated. "Does it?"

"It changes his idea of who she is," Dru said, not giving me a chance to explain. "The demon he fell in love with is more powerful and more daunting than he could have dreamed. He's intimidated, pure and simple."

"We'll work it out," I insisted. "And no, it doesn't change who I am."

We arrived at the Institute. I had alerted Amy that we were coming. She and Keisha met us in the lobby. As I antici-pated, Lucifer was in range, with Gabriel and Michael by his side.

The three archangels formed a massive wall near the elevators, talking in low voices as they watched us enter. Neve was on the phone and typing on her computer, but she took a moment to wave at me before she returned to the call. A cut on her cheek was healing, and she sported a bruise on her chin.

Bane set down the cooler on the marble floor, the tiles

gleaming from Lainie's constant polishing. I pointed to it. "It's in there," I told Keisha.

"Smells like voodoo," Vicky said.

Bane used a foot to slide it across the floor to Amy and Keisha. Amy was in jeans and a shirt with "Mom-tastic" on it. Keisha looked elegant in a teal, pink, and sunshine-yellow kaftan. Skull-and-crossbones earrings dangled to her shoulders, and she wore plum eyeliner that flicked up at the edges.

She circled the container three times clockwise, then three times counterclockwise. Her hands levitated over the top, and she made tutting noises.

Neve ended her call and peered over the edge of the desk. "What's that?"

Michael marched up. "Do you see what it did to her?" He pointed at Neve's face. "It's one thing to test me by throwing me at an unknown entity like that, but to put your friend in danger..."

"I'm fine," Neve said, giving him the stink eye. "I've handled worse ghosts than that."

Faron and Bane edged toward Lucifer and Gabriel. Dru, protectiveness rising in response to Michael's accusation, sidled up to me, his shoulder brushing mine.

I stared the archangel in the eye. "We've already had this discussion. I thought you could handle it. You *should* have been able to handle it. You're an angel, for devil's sake."

"It was exceptionally powerful," Neve said with a hint of defensiveness. "It took both of us to contain it and send it away."

"I'm sorry it hurt you." It was the truth. "I had no idea it was more than your garden variety poltergeist."

"That's just it," Michael said. "You should have known."

Fires of Hell, he was in a mood. "Check your ego, archangel. You're just upset because you encountered something that didn't bend to your will. It happens. I never know what I'm going to come up against on a case. I have to be prepared for anything."

"You know what I think?" He loomed over me, pointing a finger at my face. "I think you knew exactly what was waiting for me. It was a test, wasn't it? You wanted me to fail. You wanted to embarrass me."

Dru smacked his hand away. "Watch yourself."

Michael's icy blue eyes snapped to him. "You dare touch me?"

Neve rapped her paperweight on the top of the desk. "Enough. It wasn't a test, Michael. It was an anomaly. Kali doesn't need to embarrass you. You're quite capable of doing that all by yourself. Now, what is in that bloody cooler?"

Michael seethed. Dru stood his ground. I turned to Keisha and Amy. "It's a heart. Still beating, even though it's been cut out of the body now for several days."

Keisha wiggled her fingers at Neve. "I need chalk."

Neve opened up her pencil drawer and shook her head. "I have pens, pencils, markers..."

"A marker will do."

Neve handed her one. "That's permanent. What are you going to do?"

Keisha took it, shooed us out of the way, and dropped to her knees. She began drawing sigils and symbols in a big circle around her, chanting and singing under her breath.

"Uh-oh." Amy looked chagrined. "This can't be good. She's going to call in spirits."

Michael threw up his hands and headed for the eleva-tors. "I've had my fill of them. I'll skip this little charade."

Gabriel and Lucifer moved aside, giving him access to the buttons. He crossed his arms and stood facing the doors, while the others moved closer to watch.

Neve lifted herself partially out of her wheelchair. "I don't think that's a good idea," she said to Keisha. "Damon's not going to like permanent marker on the marble."

Amy glanced at Lucifer and back to Neve. "We'll take care of it. When she's done, we'll make sure it's erased so you don't get in trouble."

The elevator dinged as Keisha carefully lifted the heart out of the container and knelt in the circle with it. It throbbed and pulsated in her hands. She continued to chant, setting it in the center of her drawings.

Maddy and Vicky kept to themselves as they watched the exhibition.

With a flick of her wrist, Keisha sent her magic throughout all the sigils, lighting them up. The heart stut-tered, and her body seized up. Her back arched, and her eyes rolled up in her head as it snapped back. The whites of her eyes were the only thing visible in their sockets, sightless and staring at the ceiling.

Gabriel stiffened. Maddy covered her mouth and took a step back.

"Is she okay?" I asked Amy. "Should we do something?"

Words tumbled from Keisha's mouth, sounding African. Vicky tilted her head, listening carefully. Dru put a hand on my arm as if ready to jerk me away.

Amy shook her head. "She's talking to the spirits. The last thing you want to do is interrupt."

Keisha's body trembled and seized. Her head rolled around on the top of her shoulders. Her voice became someone else's, suggesting possession, and I immediately went on high alert, fearing it was Lilith. But when I moved toward her, Amy put a hand on my other arm and shook her head.

I watched in fascination, laced with dread. If it were Lilith, at least we had quite a faction gathered who could take her on.

The elevator doors opened, and everything in me was drawn toward the being who stepped out. Rad nearly knocked Michael over as he marched across the floor, stopped when he noticed us, and quickly hid the shock on his face.

It was perfect. He hadn't expected me to show up today, and it was obvious to our observers.

"What the fuck are you doing here?" he said in a low, dangerous voice.

The menace in it made Dru step in front of me with a snarl. "Talk to her like that again, and I'll make sure it's the last thing you ever say."

Lucifer's brows went up. Michael held the elevator and decided to watch the show.

Amy slipped an arm around my waist. "What's going on?"

"She's an angel, that's what's going on." Rad sidestepped Dru, pausing as he came even with him and lowered his voice. "You think you can take me, you Undead piece of shit? Give it a try."

For the second time in the past few days, a supernatural fight of epic proportions broke out, all because of me.

CHAPTER FIFTEEN

Dru was faster, but Rad was bigger. They were equally matched in skill. I tried to break it up, but the kicks, punches, and rolls happened so swiftly and with such ferocity that I wasn't sure where to dive in.

Cole came through a side door, blinked, and then continued strolling toward me. "I've got a hundred on Guitar Boy."

He barely dodged Dru's fist as the master vampire tossed Rad over his back and snarled at Cole, "You're next."

Rad landed hard, scattering Amy and Keisha. He hooked a foot around Dru's ankle and tugged, sending the vamp into a belly flop that crushed the still-beating heart under him. Michael abandoned the elevator doors and grinned as he observed the fight.

Cole had once taught me not to get in the way of a 'speeding train,' aka a fight between supernaturals. But hell, if I wasn't going to try. Jumping in the middle was impossible. Breaking them up, nearly so. The only way to stop them was to anticipate the direction they were moving and get there first.

Lucifer hustled his wife to the elevator. "Control your lovers," he snarled at me.

I was too busy moving to respond, but that didn't mean my brain didn't have a few things to say. *First of all, Dru has never been my lover. Secondly, neither of them is right now.*

He paused as I jetted past, giving me a curious glance. I snapped out both hands in a *What?* gesture.

I can hear you, he responded telepathically.

"Ugh!" I clapped my hands around my temples and missed my chance to clip Rad and Dru as they shoved their way toward Neve's desk. Maddy and Vicky scrambled behind a tall fig tree. *Get out of my head!*

You're in mine, I'm afraid to say.

Bane caught my eye with a questioning glare. Did I want help? I shook my head.

I managed to clothespin the fighting duo, my magic filling me and creating an impenetrable wall. I frowned at the fallen angel. *Wait, what?*

The elevator dinged, and Damon stepped out. He didn't even pause as he took in the destroyed lobby, the downed vampire and demon, and then me. "Did you cause this?"

Dru groaned from his spot on the floor, rubbing a hand over his face. Rad wiped blood from his nose and rolled onto his side, gasping for air. I stepped between them and Damon. "Just a misunderstanding. We'll clean things up."

Lucifer, Amy, Gabriel, and Keisha disappeared inside the elevator as the doors closed. Lucifer did not provide further explanation about his comment. *Porca miseria.* Now I had another mystery to figure out.

Cole helped Rad to his feet. Rad wouldn't look at me. Dru shrugged off my hand and rose of his own accord. Damon motioned me to the exit. "You, outside."

"Why?"

Neve wheeled herself to the smashed heart to inspect it. Faron and Bane moved toward it as well.

Damon gave me a *because I said so* glare. I gave a huff and left the others behind.

When I paused outside the doors, Damon strode past me and took the ramp to a concrete walkway that circled the second level and continued around the end of the building. Reluctantly, I followed.

The wind blew off the lake, snapping strands of my hair back. The gray blanket of sky felt close, as if I could reach out and snatch a piece of the moody clouds. The equally gray water was choppy, small breakers cresting and falling with a manic rhythm.

Damon leaned on the metal railing, staring at the water, annoyance rolling off him in waves that mimicked the lake's. Outwardly, he was the picture of calm. His magic told the real story—he was pissed.

I took a similar position, bracing my arms on the railing and watching the vast, gray roiling water. A few terns and gulls braved the gusty wind and turbulent waves, searching for food. It seemed smart to start the conversation on my own terms. "I came here seeking advice from Keisha about the heart that was left in my desk. I didn't realize Rad would be here, and had no idea he would pick a fight with Dru."

Damon said nothing for a long moment. "How many times have you observed a vampire fighting a demon?"

Weird question. "I don't know. A few?"

"Have you ever witnessed the vampire keeping his fangs retracted?"

The question threw me. Inwardly, I cringed. Had Dru given us away? I'd instructed him not to go full-on vamp when and if they fought. I hadn't even been sure they would. Because of the Omni infection, I'd been trying to make sure he didn't accidentally ingest Rad's blood. How was it possible that Damon had picked up on that?

When I didn't respond, my boss continued. "Alexandru is in love with you."

I stuttered, not expecting the conversation to go in *that* direction. "We're good friends, nothing more. You know that."

"He did not use his fangs or claws in the fight because he knows you're in love with Radison."

I turned toward him, frowning. "I'm not following."

"Inflicting a severe wound on or fatally injuring someone you love would cross a line between the two of you that could not be uncrossed. He wishes to fight for your honor, yet he knows in doing so, he could lose you forever."

Relief washed through me. Damon thought this was over a love triangle. "Are you giving me relationship advice?"

He grunted, sending a wave of his smoky demon scent my way. "In my many centuries on Earth, I have picked up a few insights."

"Yeah, well, Rad wants nothing to do with me now." I leaned heavily on the railing again, putting only as much emotion into my tone as I dared. I was Kali Sweet, after all. I didn't do emotions. "The fight was about their egos, not love."

"I cannot allow brawls to break out whenever you set foot here. You need to resolve this, and do it quickly."

I might as well play this for what it was worth. "Why does it matter that I might have angel essence mixed in with the demon? I mean, I get it—on one hand, no demon likes angels. I sure don't. But I'm still me. I'm no more about to work miracles than I am to go jump in the lake."

Damon glanced at me from the corner of his eye. "Radison will come around. Give him some time."

I peeled a strand of hair off my face. "And you? Do you feel differently about me?"

He straightened, leaving one hand on the metal railing. "I could use a drink. Let's continue this in my office."

Had I hit a sore spot? I was curious as to what he wanted to tell me, yet the fact remained that being alone with him, especially in a place teeming with his power, was a bad idea. Sharing a drink with him could turn into revealing my hand. "I wish I could, but I need to figure out my next step with Lilith. She's up to something big, and I can't figure out what. We're all vulnerable until I do."

"Did you learn anything from the heart?"

"Keisha was interrupted by the fight. I'll have to check in with her and see."

"Take Dru and leave. I'll have Keisha call you. I'll talk to Rad."

If I wasn't going to have a drink with him, he didn't even want me to go back inside. Interesting.

Truth was, I didn't want to. I did, however, want to talk to Lucifer, and he and Keisha were both in the bunker underneath us. "I can send Dru away."

Damon stared at me for a long moment, his dark eyes

searching my face for something. He knew I was keeping things from him, and a part of him was disappointed. Disheartened. I felt my own heart break a bit at the deception. "If you want to win Radison back, leave with the vampire now."

Relationship advice again. "You want me to make him jealous?"

He strode past, heading for the entrance. "What I want is irrelevant."

I stayed on his heels. "You never told me why Lilith was after you."

"She wants what she can't have." There was resignation in his voice, as if he were speaking about more than Lilith.

As if he were speaking about himself.

"Damon, if there's something you want to tell me..."

He stopped at the doors and held up a hand to stop me from entering. "When you're ready for that drink, let me know."

I started to follow him in, regardless of his indirect order, but his magic created a shield, barring me.

Speaking of crossing lines that couldn't be uncrossed—apparently, I had done so with him.

CHAPTER SIXTEEN

I waited in the idling limo for the others to emerge. Dru led the group, his dark eyes intense as he crossed the lot and climbed in next to me.

The rest of the gang followed. Bane carried the cooler, which likely held the demolished heart, and placed it in the trunk. Once everyone was settled, I instructed the driver to take us to Nudra's compound.

"Why there?" Dru asked.

"I need a car, and I want to see if Vicky can pick up on Lilith's scent."

The witch-vamp hybrid's mouth fell open. "She was there? At Nudra's? And you didn't call me?"

Thanks to Nudra, I'd inherited a host of problems—namely, her. "I found out too late to pay her a visit, and informing you of her whereabouts was not my priority."

Her lip curled, but Dru snarled, and she hastily looked away.

I had another reason to go to the Naperville estate—I

wondered if Damon had left behind surveillance equipment or tapped into the security system so he could keep an eye on me. Not that I ever visited. "Damon and his response team failed to capture her, but she may have left behind a calling card."

"She did." Dru sounded bitter. "Two dead servants."

"Not servants," I corrected. I hated the term. 'Staff.'

Corina had come and gone since Nudra's death, but she'd allowed Di to help her overcome being a former blood slave and had worked a steady job as a bartender, along with running my household.

The other member of the staff had been Barkley, a human male who'd gotten tangled up with gaming demons. They'd made him believe he was living out an apocalypse. JR had rescued him, and I'd kept him on as help.

I knew Dru was dying to ask what Damon had said to me before kicking us out. Talking about it in front of Vicky, however, might not be prudent. He was assuming it had to do with Lilith, or possibly Damon's interest in what I was hiding.

I decided to admit the truth. "It seems Damon has revoked my Bridge calling card until I have my *personal* affairs in order." I shot Dru a look. "Your fight with Rad has earned me a suspension."

His dark brows lifted, and I didn't miss Vicky's smile. "You may be the cause of the dispute, but the fight wasn't your fault. It was Rad's."

I chuckled. "At least have the balls to admit you played a part in it." He gave a dashing grin. I shrugged. "Damon still wants Lilith sent to Hell, but he seems less likely to trust me to get the job done."

Vicky snorted. "He's not the only one."

Faron sent me a sympathetic look. Bane appeared pissed. About what, who knew, but that seemed to be his standard mode, so I wasn't too worried about it.

We arrived at the estate and drove through the gates to the side entrance. Before allowing anyone inside, I placed my hand on the building and sent my magic spiraling into it to check for uninvited guests.

Earth magic flowed up through my feet and legs, flooding my system and waking my demon. She sighed as if sinking into a warm tub of water, and I sent another pulse of magic into the structure.

Lilith had corrupted the energy inside. What she'd done was different than Nudra's past escapades, but this held demonic energy. The phantom scent of sulfur and fire filled my nose, and my demon snapped out her claws. While she craved the power Lilith wielded, she saw her as a threat.

The others in our party gathered around. I could feel their conflicting magic signatures tickling my back. Curiosity mingled with impatience, but this wasn't something I was willing to hurry.

After a moment of riding the waves of Lilith's imprint, I shifted my magic to search for Damon's.

Only a trace zipped along my spine, but this, too, snagged my demon's attention. Her threat assessment shifted as she welcomed his energy, drawing it up like she was sipping through a straw.

The spirits of the dead called to me. Not only the two staff members Lilith had killed, but also those Nudra had tormented and drained of blood during his time in residence. Hundreds of them—all denied peace—screamed in my ears.

With a gasp, I stepped back, dropping my hand. *That* had never happened before.

Dru touched my lower back. "What is it?"

"I need to get Neve here to put some spirits to rest. But not today." I went to the door and held it open. "Come on."

The place resembled a frat house after a Saturday night party. Remnants of food, plates, cups, takeout boxes, and bags were strewn across the kitchen and dining rooms. More debris had been left in the living areas and pool room. Clothes, shoes, books, and knick-knacks had been ripped apart, chewed on, smashed, and set on fire.

There were holes in the walls, burn marks in the carpeting, and gouges in the doors. Ceiling lights had been ripped down, curtains and blinds yanked from windows. The scents of sulfur and sex hung in the air.

Bane whistled under his breath. Faron made a face at a pool of blood. The bodies had been removed, thanks to Damon's team, but the remnants of what had happened to them—and whoever else Lilith had invited for the party—were evident everywhere.

Maddy checked the refrigerator, helping herself to one of the only remaining sodas. "Looks like Lilith had fun."

Vicky inhaled deeply, her eyes fluttering closed for a moment. "Sacrifices were made."

"Leaving behind quite a message," Dru said.

Faron nodded in agreement. "This was systematic destruction, symbolizing what she's trying to do to you."

My phone rang. Seeing who it was, I left the group to answer it. "Did you get anything?" I asked Keisha.

"Zeus Hayden. That's what the spirits told me."

"Is he the owner of the heart, or the one who cut it out?"

"The latter. His imprint is on the heart itself. I did a search, and there are two in the area with that name, believe it or not. I'm sending you their addresses."

"So, he's into voodoo?"

"This wasn't voodoo. This was necromancy." At my pause, she continued. "Both are used for divination, but voodoo is a spiritual system using ancestor veneration and the interaction with those spirits for guidance and assistance. Like what you saw me do at the Institute."

"Still looks like necromancy to me."

"Necromancy is a tool used by some religious and spiritual practitioners to gain information in a similar way to influence the living, predict the future, and even to raise the dead to manipulate them or future events. Necromancy isn't a religion, nor does it focus on ancestors."

How textbook. "I get that. How can you be positive that this wasn't one of your practitioners who carved out the heart and kept it beating?"

"Because Zeus is a vampire. While there are a few of them who practice my religion, I'd bet my most powerful juju bag he's using necromancy. It fits with the whole Undead thing. The person the heart came from is probably a walking zombie."

Lovely. "Thanks for your help."

We disconnected, and I turned to find Faron behind me. Good. "Did you get anything from the angels while we were there?" I asked.

"Only that Lucifer was shocked you could project comments into his mind. How did you do that, by the way?"

I rubbed my forehead and pocketed the phone. "Not a

clue. Did you pick up on any deceit among them regarding what they've told me about the Omnis?"

"None. I had to be careful digging around inside their heads. As you can imagine, they are exceptionally perceptive about such things."

That was good and bad. It either confirmed that they were truthful in their dealings with me, or that they had buried the truth so far down that even the Fate couldn't decipher it without alerting them that she was poking around in their cerebral matter.

Cole texted me, complaining that I had stolen his hundred dollars. He had a couple of hours off and wanted to meet at the local demon bar to pick a fight with someone. Did I want in?

That Cole—always thinking of me.

The addresses came through from Keisha, so I forwarded them to him, asking him to meet me at the closest one in thirty minutes. He responded with a thumbs-up.

I rounded up the gang. "We're heading to a penthouse in Lincoln Park."

"For what?" Dru asked.

"To hunt a vampire."

Maddy clapped her hands. "Hot damn."

Dru's forehead creased. "Who is it?"

"Zeus Hayden. Heard of him?"

The crease grew deeper. "The millionaire?"

"He's in your nest. I assume you know."

"He owed a strong allegiance to Nudra. He hasn't shown the same deference to me."

I patted his shoulder. "Let's go change that."

He grabbed my hand. "We don't go to a subordinate, my Queen. They come to us."

Maddy snickered. Vicky heaved a dramatic sigh and gave him a flat look. "If he's blown you off before, what makes you think he'll come at your beck and call now?"

Dru gave a rueful smile. "I'm not the one summoning him." He brushed a kiss across the top of my knuckles, a lock of his dark hair falling across his forehead as he looked at me from beneath it. "His Queen is."

CHAPTER SEVENTEEN

Dru sent Maddy to Hayden's high-rise office building with a message. He was expected at the Chicago House at midnight sharp.

I wanted to add a threat to accompany that message, but Dru said it was implied. While Hayden had avoided his responsibilities, a direct summons could not be dismissed. The vampire blood that ran in his veins would compel him to cooperate, overriding his own will.

Cole was disappointed he didn't get to beat somebody up for me, but I made him happy when I suggested we go hunting for a primordial demon.

He rubbed his hands together. "As long as I'm back at the Institute by dinner. Lainie promised me roasted lamb tonight."

Dinner time at the Institute was ten. "Shouldn't be a problem."

I offered the others the option to bail if any had other responsibilities or duties to perform. It was also a way to let them off the hook if they were as frustrated as I was about our lack of success so far.

None of them, not even Dru, took the bait. Whether it was out of loyalty to me or the driving desire to catch Lilith, they all seemed as determined as I was to put that bitch in her place.

Fright Night was a trendy club I'd visited more than once, chasing supernaturals who'd stepped over the line with humans. It was early for the typical house music crowd, who wouldn't arrive until well after sunset, but the person I needed to speak to should have time for my questions.

Hone, a cross between a Hawaiian fire dancer and a pro wrestler, was the most sought-after and highly paid bouncer in Chicago. Hone had been my muscle on many jobs—some for the Bridge and just as many for Sweet Investigations.

He could've easily played for the Bears, but his true gift was the fact he could read minds. That's what made him excel at his job. He knew what people were going to do before they did it, and therefore, he could outwit any idiot stupid enough to start a fight and cause trouble.

It had been weeks since I'd last checked in with him, and after seeing how Lilith had trashed my Naperville house, I'd had an idea. Even though she was playing passive-aggressive by avoiding me while still taunting me, she hadn't left Chicago. Her appetites were insatiable, and Fright Night offered her a smorgasbord to feast on.

Bass music thumped behind the brick walls, a line already forming at the door. As I marched to the front, some of the crowd grumbled and threw out insults. One look from Dru, Cole, and Bane, and the disgruntled shut their mouths and glanced away as Hone greeted me. "Kali Sweet, as I live and die." He pulled me in for a hug, nearly suffocating me against his chest. "Whachyou doin' here?"

I patted his gigantic bicep and took a step back as he released me. "Looking for a friend."

His lips pursed, and he looked as if he were in pain. "Yeah, he was here last night."

He? "Who?"

"Rad. He put on quite a show."

I exchanged glances with Cole. "Did you know about this?"

He shook his head. "What kind of show?"

Hone frowned as if we were both dense. "On stage?" He pulled out his phone, tapped it a couple of times, and showed us the screen. "It's all over social media. I figured y'saw it. What did you do to that poor guy, Kali? Even in all the years he was with the Chaos Demons, I never heard him sound so...wrecked."

While Fright Night mostly hosted hot DJs from around the area, it occasionally brought in popular bands as well. On screen, Rad was being coerced on stage and handed a guitar. He seemed reluctant to step up to the mic, but the cheers from the crowd were an encouragement. They began chanting, "Beaumont, Beaumont, Beaumont."

He closed his eyes for a moment, and when he reopened them, I saw the rock god he used to be. He strummed the guitar once, and the crowd fell silent, a spell coming over them.

Maddy, Dru, and Faron pressed in around me, watching over my shoulders as we, too, became mesmerized. Rad's voice came out clear, yet ragged. Haunted. The song he sang was one he'd written for me. *Whisper in the Dark*. I knew the words by heart.

> *Listen to my music*
> *Listen to my heart*
> *Find the good within*
> *What's lost is keeping us apart*

I FINALLY FOUND *my way*
> *No words of mine can ever say*
> *How much I miss you...*

MY GUT TIGHTENED. Cole snickered. Maddy placed a hand on my lower back in support.

"What the fuck was he doing here?" I muttered under my breath.

It wasn't until then that Hone noticed Vicky. His hand holding the phone dropped to his side. "What the fuck is *she* doing here?"

Not that long ago, when Vicky was still a witch, she'd attacked Hone while he guarded her and put him in the hospital. He was a teddy bear underneath all that muscle, but he didn't forget or forgive. If you crossed him the wrong way, you were his enemy for life.

I put a hand on his chest. "She's helping us hunt down the friend I was telling you about. Not Rad." My heart felt all discombobulated after seeing him on stage. I knew this was all an act, but why did it feel so real? "Lilith. She's topside again, and she's causing a lot of trouble. Fright Night is the perfect place for her to hunt."

Hone continued to zero in on Vicky, and although she was typically smug and didn't back down from any of us, she was smart enough to stay out of his reach. "You better be thankful Kali is here." He leaned into my hand, as if ready to go after her anyway. Not with any true force, but definitely with an imminent threat in his eyes. "Otherwise, I would tear you apart and then toss you in Lake Michigan for the fish."

Dru smiled, flashing his fangs. "That could still be arranged."

Vicky said nothing. She just stood there, trying to act bored.

"I should've told you," Maddy said, close to my ear. "I saw that video, and about a hundred more filmed from the crowd. Everyone's asking if Rad is making a comeback."

My heart squeezed. I shoved away the emotions. This wasn't the time or place. And while he'd given up his music career for me, he seemed happy. Wasn't he?

Seeing him on that stage performing an impromptu song made me realize how much he missed it.

I brought out my own phone and showed Hone pictures of Lilith. "She has the ability to change her appearance, but she rarely does. She likes the original and is too vain to change it. Any chance you've seen her?"

He tore his gaze away from Vicky to study my screen. "Maybe." He shook his head. "I can't be sure. I see hundreds of people every night."

"Any chance we could check your security footage?" Cole asked.

Hone scanned the growing lineup and pocketed his

phone. He unhooked one end of the thick, black cord that crossed the entrance. "Go on in. I'll see what I can do."

We filed past, hearing the disgruntled comments from those in line, but he stopped Vicky before she could pass. "Not you."

"You and I want the same thing," she said. "To help Kali."

He paused for a moment, and I knew he was reading her mind. Surprisingly, she must've let him. As a vampire, she could block him out, but she must've realized it was in her best interest not to.

Whatever he discovered there, it must have satisfied him. He stepped sideways and cocked his chin for her to join us. "One time. This is your one and only free pass, you feel me?"

She didn't answer, hustling to catch up with us as we entered the club.

I spotted a dozen demons, vampires, and other creatures mixing with the humans who gyrated to the music. I noted another dozen humans preying on other humans.

I wished I had my old cloak so I could put up the hood and block them out, every cell in my supernatural body wanting to protect the innocent and gullible ripe for their attention. However, I no longer had that cloak, and that wasn't my mission tonight.

I led our conga line toward the rear of the place, nodding at the bartender as we passed, who was a good friend of Chloe's, the tempter demon who ran the local blood bank. He nodded back and gestured at the lineup of booze behind him with a questioning lift of one brow. I shook my head and waved him off.

Hone worked his way past the crowd to get ahead of me and open the door to the security room. We followed him up a flight of steps and dropped in on a young, skinny human in cargo shorts and a T-shirt three days past needing a wash. He was watching a couple of male vampires close up on one of the dozens of screens in front of him while he crammed his face with Cheetos.

When he saw us, he came up out of his seat too fast, knocking the Cheetos everywhere and blubbering. We squeezed into the tiny room, and Hone knocked the kid on the back of the head when he saw he'd been getting off on watching the vampires. The tent in the front of his pants confirmed he wasn't taking security too seriously.

"Hone." He tried to gather up the fallen Cheetos and wipe off his fingers on his pants. In the process, he noticed he was sporting an erection and quickly turned away from us. "What's up? I was just, uh..."

Hone hitched a thumb over his massive shoulder. "Get out of here."

The kid placed his orange-stained fingers in front of his crotch and glanced around at all of us. "My shift ain't over, and I don't think they're supposed to be in here, are they?"

Hone grabbed him by the lapels and threw him out, slamming the door behind him. "*Hupo*," he muttered under his breath. I didn't know much Hawaiian, but I knew that meant idiot.

He shoved the abandoned chair to the side and fiddled with the keyboard. While most of the screens continued to depict the present group of folks on the floor, at the bar, and in the private viewing rooms above the dance floor, he managed to bring up the previous evening's recording on the center screen. The timestamp began at nine p.m.

"It runs for six hours." Hone glanced over his shoulder at me. "You gonna sit here and watch the whole thing?"

All I wanted to watch was Rad's performance, but I kept that to myself. I'd replay it later in the privacy of my place since it was apparently all over the Internet. "Knowing Lilith, she wouldn't show up until midnight or after, and she would probably cause a scene of some sort, like a queen ruling over her court."

"I know what to look for," Vicky interjected. She grabbed the chair to pull it back in front of the desk. "I'll stay and scan the footage."

"Not on your own," Hone said.

Bane leaned against the wall, crossing his arms. "We'll stay with her."

Faron gave him a questioning look. "We will?"

Bane jutted his chin to one of the other screens. "Look who's on the dance floor. We should keep an eye on him."

All of our gazes followed his. Faron released a heavy sigh. "Tromble Lope."

"Who's that?" Vicky asked.

Bane's countenance matched his gruff reply. "A necromancer we've had a few skirmishes with."

I'd had more than one run-in with him as well. He was fascinated with the Undead and played around with the *actual* dead, but always managed to avoid the Bridge's wrath.

I raised an eyebrow at Faron, and she nodded. She and Bane would babysit Vicky and see if Lilith had made an appearance at the club the previous night. I wasn't sure how that would help me track her down, but if I could see who she interacted with, it might be a lead. A slim one, but that was all I had at this point. I thanked Hone and gathered the others.

We dropped Cole at the Institute, and Dru, Maddy, and I went to the House to prepare for our visitor.

As Dru had claimed, Zeus arrived promptly at the designated time. Like most vampires, he sported an unnatural beauty, with dark skin, eerie golden eyes, and a set of braids that made me jealous. His face was sharp, his nose sharper.

He bowed deeply to me in Dru's office and spoke with a distinct British accent. "My Queen." He reached to take my hand to kiss my knuckles, but I wouldn't allow it, and he withdrew politely. "How may I be of service?"

CHAPTER EIGHTEEN

I wasn't one to beat around the bush. "What have you been up to, Zeus? Do you enjoy removing the hearts of your victims while they're still beating?"

His gaze had been lowered, but now it snapped up to mine. His head cocked slightly. "Pray tell, I don't understand."

"The calling card you left in my desk drawer. A pretty fancy trick, keeping the heart beating after it's been removed from the body."

He stepped back, placing one hand over his heart, as if I'd wounded him. His aura was a similar gold to his eyes, and it flared orange at the accusation. "I assure you, I have done no such thing. I follow the Chicago House rules of conduct. I don't have 'victims,' and I certainly don't go about removing their hearts. Besides, I don't even know where your office is. And why would I do such a thing?"

I sat on the edge of the desk, crossing my legs at the ankles. "Cut the bullshit. I know you're taking orders from

Lilith. What I don't understand is why she would have you deliver the heart to my office and leave it in my desk. Also, a huge security breach, so my IT guy is looking into that. She's not typically passive-aggressive. She's more in your face with a red-hot poker."

Another cock of his head in the other direction. "Who is this Lilith?"

I didn't see the tell-tale flicker of brown that often flared in someone's aura when lying. Which only meant he was a good actor. "You know who she is. Tell me where I can find her, and we'll let this indiscretion go, tacking it up to you being influenced by a demon you couldn't say no to."

His brow became a ridge across his face as he frowned. He looked down at the floor, then at Dru. "Master, I assure you I do not understand what she's talking about." Those golden eyes flicked back to me. "Are you saying Lilith, the mother of *demons*, forced me to take a heart from someone and place it in your office desk?"

"That's exactly what I'm saying. We know you did it."

He shook his head adamantly. "And I know that I did not. Your information is wrong."

Dru and I exchanged glances. Dru could read his mind and know if he was lying. He gave a subtle shake of his head to signal that Zeus wasn't.

Which confirmed what I saw in his aura.

Dammit. Was Keisha wrong?

I paced behind Zeus, invading his personal space to make him squirm. He didn't, but I picked up on a faint odor I hadn't before. "Show me your hands," I ordered.

With a tight flick of his eyes in my direction, he held them out, palms up. "I do not understand any of this."

I didn't want to touch him, but I didn't have to. There, on his left wrist, was the Fright Night club emblem peeking out from under the cuff of his sleeve.

The stamps were iridescent, not obvious, but they showed up under the right light. I perched on the edge of Dru's desk again. The scent I'd caught on Zeus was the club's signature incense. "When was the last time you were at the club?"

He jerked slightly. "Club?"

"Fright Night. You have a stamp."

Dru sat up slowly, like a predator, and Zeus tensed. "I'm allowed to go there. As always, and as I've already mentioned, I abide by the rules of the House. I have not violated Bridge Laws. I'm not hunting when I go there, just enjoying myself."

That was probably also true. "When was your last visit?"

A heavy, aggrieved sigh. "Last night."

"You're a regular?"

Another flash of his golden eyes. "I wouldn't say that, but I frequent it when I'm in town."

"And ignore your duties to the House," Dru put in.

Zeus lowered his hands. "Shall I make reparations, Master?"

A glint shone in Dru's dark eyes. "We'll discuss those once your queen has finished with her questions."

The floor was mine again. "When visiting Fright Night, have you seen a drop-dead gorgeous woman collecting friends?"

His pause was brief but telling. "There are many women at the club who meet that description."

This was getting me nowhere. "Why would your magical

fingerprint be on the heart that ended up in my desk, if you didn't have anything to do with it?"

His frustration soared. He made a gesture of helplessness. "I have no idea. I'm not into females, so it's not like I accidentally took a demon home for a hook-up and she stole my vampire DNA."

Thoughts swirled in my head. "Who *have* you hooked up with recently?"

His backbone straightened. "I hardly think that's any of your business."

Dru practically came out of his seat. "Answer your queen."

I felt his magic and the compulsion that he forced onto Zeus. It bit into my skin, rattled my bones.

Zeus swayed on his feet, nearly collapsing. "I meet someone on occasion there."

"Who?" I demanded.

"He's not human—not really—and I never drain him."

Dru bore down on him. "What's his name?"

He opened his mouth to reply, but I already knew what he was going to say. "Tromble," we both said at the same time.

"The necromancer," I clarified.

Dru stepped back. "Why in the name of blood would you hook up with such a being?"

Zeus gave me a pointed look as if throwing the question back at his master about me. In some ways, it was a fair point. Demons and vampires hated each other. The fact that I was queen of the region contradicted all their principles.

"You've been very helpful," I told him. It wasn't exactly true, but getting to Tromble, and therefore to Lilith, might depend on what else Zeus could provide. "I need to talk to your friend. Can you arrange a meeting for me?"

Relief that he was no longer under suspicion, but wariness about turning in his lover, set up a healthy conflict behind his eyes. "Is he in trouble for this?"

Of course, he was, but if I admitted that, I wouldn't get very far with Zeus. "My guess is he's been manipulated by Lilith. In that case, he can't be held accountable for his actions. He may not even realize that she's using him. This is your chance to protect him."

I might not be a vampire, but I could often push on another's buttons and motivate them to do what I wanted just as easily. If I didn't know better, I would think Zeus was actually in love with the guy. I doubted Tromble felt the same way. Zeus was most likely his latest experiment, and he was collecting the vampire's DNA as often as possible for his scientific studies.

It technically wasn't against Bridge mandates, since it was a consensual relationship. Still, if the necromancer was using the vampire's DNA inappropriately, for whatever experiments he might be doing, that was a different story.

Thing was, what I told Zeus was a possibility. Tromble might not even realize that he was under Lilith's spell.

Either way, this gave me a solid lead to pursue. I grabbed my phone and sent a text to Faron, asking if Tromble was still at the club. I didn't want her to spook him, but it might be prudent to have her keep an eye on him until I could return.

"May I go now?" the vampire asked.

The moment I let him vanish, he might alert his lover that I was looking for him, and all of this would be for nothing. I turned to Dru. "I'm done with my questioning, but I believe you have some items to go over with Zeus?"

He did, but he also picked up on my cue to keep the vampire engaged. "We have multiple things to discuss." He pointed at one of the visitor chairs. "Sit."

Zeus glanced toward the door, as if he might try to make a break for it. He was too smart for that, knowing he wouldn't get far, and that he'd be in far more trouble. With resigned annoyance, he lowered himself into the chair stiffly.

My phone pinged, and I wiggled it in the air. "I need to take this. I'll catch up with you in a bit."

I could see that Dru didn't like being left out of whatever I was planning, but he gave a nod, and I slipped out the door.

In the lavish hallway, with its plush carpeting and high ceiling, I read Faron's reply. *He left an hour ago. Why?*

I headed down the immense staircase, swearing quietly under my breath. Several vampires passed by, dipping their heads in respect. I messaged her back. *Where is his current hole? Do you have an address?*

Thought bubbles appeared, and then her message. *In the tunnels under the Kinzie Street Bridge. Meet you there?*

Good. That gave me what I needed. I thumbs-upped the note and flew out the front door of the mansion.

Maybe I'd find more than the necromancer in the tunnels. Maybe I'd find Lilith.

CHAPTER NINETEEN

The bridge and the area around it were quiet. It took a few minutes to find the entrance to the tunnels, and my nose scrunched at the rancid smell. Even though it was winter, flies were everywhere.

Using my magic, I drew a protective bubble around myself and flicked on my internal night vision. One of the latest gifts my growing magic had acquired. I wasn't sure if it was vampire, angel, or Omni. Didn't matter. I had it and I used it.

As I descended through the underground pathways, the air grew thick with dampness and the scent of mildew, mixed with a sharpness of discarded metal, body odor, and old food wrappers.

I passed broken appliances, filthy mattresses, random clothes, and junkie needles. Here and there were makeshift firepits, all cold, and signs of domestication—curtains hung on pipes to form rooms, plates and cups stacked in corners. A few spots had oil lamps and flashlights, rusting on forgotten tables.

Graffiti decorated the concrete ribs of the passageways. Most of it was cartoonish, but a few gang symbols had been spray-painted in concentration in several areas. Yet I didn't meet a single living person. Not even a rat.

Too cold? The temperature was dropping below freezing tonight. My breath frosted in clouds as I walked.

I didn't find any dead bodies. No bones. I couldn't decide if that was good or bad.

The deeper I went, the more my demon perked up. While I didn't detect the recent use of magic in any of the places I ventured through, she twanged like a tight guitar string when I came to a cavernous chamber where several tunnels intersected.

The walls here were lined with binding runes that pulsed a sickly green color. Stubs of black candles anchored points for a huge pentagram in the center of the floor. The flies were worse, even though there were no dead bodies.

Necromantic magic slid over my bubble and turned my stomach queasy as if Death himself was reaching in to twist it. My nose caught the scent of graveyard dirt, and a few ghosts, tethered to the floor, floated in place, watching me. "Here you are, necromancer," I murmured.

I walked the circumference of the pentagram, making sure not to touch its lines. Inside each section was a sigil, a word, a drawing. My nearness to it made the ghosts moan and writhe.

Other shadows clung close, reeking of demon magic. I kept my wards strong, mostly because I didn't want to get tangled up with whatever necromantic magic Tromble was experimenting with. While I didn't care for the idiot, I was here for a much bigger fish.

Unfortunately, without him, I had no source to point me in Lilith's direction. This was a waste of time.

Scanning the tethered souls and the demonic shadows, I wondered which one I could yank on to get the necromancer's attention without ending up hooked into them. *Ding-dong, you've got company.*

Was it worth it? The last thing I needed was to end up with a hitchhiker, especially if poking the bear got me nowhere with my mission.

I still wasn't one hundred percent sure that the heart was Lilith's calling card. Nor was I sure about how she'd possessed Rad. I'd dealt with her enough in the past to be quite familiar with her tactics. Something about all of this seemed off.

Still debating about whether to risk engaging with one of the ghosts, I tensed when a creeping sensation ran down the back of my neck and slammed into the base of my spine.

I whirled. A glow illuminated the cavernous space as Michael appeared, bringing all his angelic light with him. Squeezing my eyes shut, I turned off my night vision before reopening them.

Dressed in ratty jeans and a leather jacket, his thick, wavy blonde hair was elegantly messy. He could have posed for a commercial—he'd used enough product in it and had probably spent an hour in front of the mirror making it model-perfect.

Under the leather jacket was a band T-shirt—the Chaos Demons' last European tour. The black motorcycle boots on his feet had spikes and chains.

I snorted. "Did you let Maddy give you a makeover?"

His lips quirked. "Are you kidding? She would've turned me into a Goth." He spun a full three-sixty, flaring out his hands like a supermodel. "Di did this. What do you think?"

Thanks to his magic, the ghosts squirmed and thrashed like dancers moving to a techno beat, desperate to break free from their tethers in order to get away from him. The demonic shadows disappeared into the walls and floor. None of them seemed to like Michael's presence.

They weren't the only ones. "It's better than a golf shirt and khakis."

A finger pointed at the ghosts. "Didn't take you for a ghost girl."

"Why don't you send them to the other side? You could use the practice."

A snicker. "No thanks. Call Neve." He glanced at the pentagram. "Why are you trying to summon a demon?"

"This isn't my artwork. It belongs to a necromancer who I think might have ties to Lilith."

He bent down to examine the sigils. "Why would Lilith summon a demon using a pentagram? She doesn't need that type of portal."

"Don't touch it," I cautioned. "It may be booby-trapped. I have no idea why she's using a necromancer, or what she's trying to do here, but a lot of things she does don't make sense."

I brought him up to speed about Zeus and his connection to Tromble. "Lilith has her moments of being passive-aggressive, but the heart, as well as her messing up my house in Naperville, seems petty, even for her. Plus, I can't figure out why she was messing around with possessing

Rad in order to get to Damon. What does she want with him?"

"Speaking of your boss, he's a real dick these days. He acts like someone killed his puppy. I think it's all because of you."

"He's always been moody, but he's always had my back until now."

"For some reason, he's convinced Lucifer and I have brainwashed you into helping us with some plot to take over the world. I'm pretty surprised he hasn't kicked us out of the Institute like he did you."

"He believes in keeping his enemies close," I said.

He shrugged. "The guy is seriously depressed. I think he regrets banning you."

I usually understood Damon's motives and actions. Kicking me out, however, didn't make sense. "I guess he's decided that if you're going to brainwash me into helping you with your evil schemes, he's not allowing it to happen under his roof."

The archangel stood, shoving his hands into his pockets and pacing around the circumference of the pentagram. It had probably been decades, if not longer, since the space had seen so much light. "If Lilith weren't already walking the Earth, I'd say your necromancer is trying to raise her. The sigils inside this thing are powerful. Big guns. You don't use these for summoning lower-level demons."

And the demons currently hiding in the walls weren't that powerful. That's why they hadn't attacked me and had scurried off when Michael arrived. "So this portal could be used to raise, say, an archdemon? Like Damon?"

"Possibly." He glanced around. "What's with all the

flies?" Then his eyes widened, snapping back to the penta-gram. "Holy sacrament."

"What?"

"I think I know who they're trying to summon."

Footsteps sounded in the tunnel, and I put a finger to my lips to silence him. We both moved to the sides of the entrance, concealing ourselves, even though there was no hiding his light.

"Kali?"

Rad's voice echoed in the space, and my shoulders relaxed. I left my hiding spot and met him at the entrance. "In here."

He looked good enough to eat. My demon licked her lips. It had barely been twenty-four hours, and she was already desperate to jump his bones. I didn't blame her. He put Michael, in all of his badass makeover glory, to shame. "Damn," he said. "Glad I found you."

"What are you doing here?"

He was about to reach for me when he noticed the archangel, now leaning his shoulder against the stone wall. The angel lifted a hand in greeting and then pulled aside his jacket lapel to reveal his T-shirt. "Hey, man."

Rad's lips firmed before his gaze swung back to me. "I assume we're all here for the same reason. Lilith?"

I touched his arm, unable to resist as I moved closer to him. My eyes feasted on his face, his broad shoulders, his lean waist. "Did you follow her here?"

He closed the distance between us and scooped me around the waist to pull me to him. My breasts pressed into his chest, and he lowered his mouth so it was only a few centimeters from mine as he stared into my eyes. "I didn't follow her. I followed you."

Heat erupted low in my belly. I grabbed him by the back of the neck and kissed him. I would've kept doing it, too, even with the ghosts and the flies and that stupid pentagram, if not for Michael clearing his throat.

We broke apart, both of us breathing hard. My voice came out in a husky rush. "Why are you following me?"

He touched his forehead to mine. "What kind of male would I be if I didn't watch your back?"

I toyed with a lock of his hair, grinning. He was only saying that because he knew it would irritate me. Deep down, it actually pleased me, which irritated me more. "Damon told you to keep tabs on me, didn't he? He figured I was your best bet to find Lilith."

Rad chuckled. "Can't get anything past you, can we?"

Michael cleared his throat again. "Hate to break up this reunion, kids, but you're not going to like what this is leading to."

Once more, we were interrupted.

"Well, look at this," a feminine voice dripping with all the deadly sins said as she appeared before us. "The gang's all here."

Lilith's magic hit me so hard, it knocked me on my ass and sent me skidding across the stone floor, straight into the pentagram.

Before the other two could react, she stepped up to Rad and wrapped her arms around one of his, laying her head on his shoulder. "Let's get this party started, shall we?"

CHAPTER TWENTY

The pentagram flared a bright red, engulfing me and most of the floor in a deadly trap.

I jumped to my feet, opening my palm for Volante's hilt, but realized too late that she'd been ripped from my arm. She lay in a heap near Michael's feet, and he reached for her at the same time Rad tried to shove Lilith away.

Her claws emerged and locked onto his neck. "Do what I tell you to do, or Kali goes bye-bye."

The pentagram wasn't for *summoning* demons; it was for sending one in particular—me—to hell.

Volante morphed into Michael's blazing sword. Snatching it up, he faced Lilith, blue flames licking the blade, but she only smiled. "Run along, little angel, this doesn't concern you."

I swore loudly and violently. I'd fallen into her trap. A clever one, too. Guess payback really was a bitch, since I'd done something similar to her in the graveyard behind my home not that long ago.

"Poetic," I said, keeping my eye on her and Rad through the red blaze of the ward. His eyes locked on mine, the cords in his neck standing out as her claws dug deep.

Blood trickled from the wounds. I needed to distract her fast to get her away from him. He was my weakness, and she knew it. "Did you come up with this plan on your own, Lil, or did you have help?"

She hated being called any nickname, and her top lip curled as she started to reply.

Before she could, Michael cut in. "Oh, she had help. Where is he?" He glanced around the space, the flaming sword held at the ready. "It's not like him to hide."

"Who?" I demanded.

Michael flicked his eyes to me, back to her. "I believe they call him Ba'al Zebub."

My stomach dropped. No. Way.

Known in many religions and by many different names and titles, he was a true prince of Hell—the ruler long before Lucifer pissed off Daddy and usurped him.

While in many myths Ba'al was one of the three most prominent fallen angels that included Lucifer, the truth was he'd never been an angel. Known as The King of Flying Demons, shortened in some human translations to the King of Flies, he was an original who embodied all seven deadly sins.

A true supreme monarch of Hell, known for corrupting individuals and societies, shapeshifting, and capable of causing widespread destruction and chaos, he was legendary.

Keeping the sword aloft, Michael slid closer to the penta-gram and gave me a headshake, but spoke to Lilith. "I don't think he's been topside in what, a few thousand years? If you've raised him, that's an impressive feat."

"He and I go way back," she said, unconcerned with the sword. "We're some of the originals, you know."

That's when the idea struck—the originals, like Lilith, Adam, and the serpent, were all living it up in Eden until the whole apple debacle introduced sin. Now, here we were, still fighting over who got what when it came to humans.

But the Omnis...they were originals, too, weren't they? The *original* originals.

Lilith released Rad, and I saw his shoulders relax a fraction. He tried to move, but his eyes widened and met mine. He seemed to be frozen in place.

Of course, he was. That's why she was unconcerned about any revolt from him when she faced Michael, eyes lingering on his proximity to the pentagram. "He's one of my favorite deities, and he owes me a favor."

My memory flashed back to Rad behind the prison bars. We thought it was possession, but it was Ba'al Zebub, who loved chaos and shapeshifting.

Rad had been the ideal container for him and Lilith to test for whatever plan they had.

I glanced down at the outline of the pentagram. There was no way I was going to Hell. I feared Michael touching the pentagram with the sword might backfire—which I was sure was his plan—but it also might be the only chance I had. If his angelic fire could break even one of the lines, the spell would dissolve. I'd be free again. "What favor is that?" I asked, hoping to distract her.

She flicked her wrist, her nails flicking droplets of Rad's

blood onto the floor. Her voice purred, and her eyes gleamed. "Doesn't matter. What does matter is that I have you."

At least I had her attention on me. "Why don't you step inside this pentagram with me and let's have it out? Best demon wins."

A soft chuckle escaped her lips, painted a deep red. "We all know who the best demon is. That's why you're in the pentagram and I'm not."

"I know you're upset about me betraying you, but the angels made me a better deal. You can't blame me for looking out for myself. I *am* a demon, after all."

The gleam in her eyes went flat. "You accepted a contract from Victoria to hunt me down."

"The Bridge Institute already wanted your head. I was going to hunt you down either way. Why wouldn't I capitalize on Vicky's anger at what you had done to her?"

Lilith's demeanor hardened even more. "She was supposed to be the sacrifice."

Keeping her talking allowed me to examine the sigils as I paced. I had a knack for dismantling demon traps, and although this one was more like a vault, I knew it had weaknesses. Every trap did. "Sacrifice to Ba'al Zebub? I thought he owed you a favor. Why would you need a sacrifice for him?"

The red haze of the ward brightened, as if in response to some emotion churning through her. "Try not to strain your stupid little head, *alciscor*. To raise a supreme being from Hell, one must provide a proper sacrifice."

I chuckled. "I hardly think Vicky is a proper sacrifice for anything. Damon, on the other hand..." I tilted my head. "Is that why you were trying to get to him?"

She glanced at Michael, then at Rad. The ward dimmed. Was it tied to her emotions? "I'm now in charge of Chicago," she informed me. "I have your boyfriend, your possessions, and soon I'll have the angels and demons bowing to me. I'm bringing a whole new hellscape to earth."

"You're delusional." Michael lowered the blade slightly, a frown creasing his brow. "You don't have the power to do that."

She sauntered back to Rad, brushing a hand across his broad shoulders and giving Michael and me a wicked grin. "I may not have before, but I do now."

Because she'd raised an original. One who supposedly owed her a favor.

I sent my demon pummeling into the stone ground underneath me, pulling up as much Earth energy as I could. The floor shook as everyone scrambled to find their footing. Lilith grabbed Rad to steady herself and curled that lip again to hiss at me. "What are you doing?"

All I needed to do was crack a sigil. I pulled up more magic, giving my demon everything she wanted. She arched inside of me, soaking it up, and pieces of the ceiling began to fall from the quake. Lilith screamed, but it was cut short when Rad, now free from her spell, withdrew a gleaming silver blade and jammed it into her heart.

I hadn't expected that, and I certainly didn't expect what happened next. Lilith, those red lips parted and eyes wide with shock, dropped to her knees. Rad kept the blade buried in her chest as she did so. She gripped his arms, sinking her claws in deep with one hand as she tried to extract the blade with the other.

Her magic whirled within the cavern, the ward turning

blood red, as it tightened and tried to squeeze me. But Rad's chaos magic rose with a fury and buffeted it. It also drove the blade in so deeply that the tip protruded from her back.

Michael lunged forward and brought the sword down, cleaving Lilith nearly in half and barely missing Rad. Her body spasmed, another scream erupted from her throat, and then...

The mother of demons exploded into ashes.

The ward collapsed, and the ground beneath my feet split open in a jagged expanse. The sigils disintegrated and the candles toppled. Their flames went out, and they rolled across the floor, several of them dropping into the chasm opening near my feet.

I jumped aside and started to cross the closest line of the broken trap, mesmerized by the falling ash that had just been one of my greatest adversaries, when a monster appeared right in front of me.

The thing was massive, taller than Michael, with horns curling on either side of his head. His snout was shaped like a goat's, and his tongue, which he flicked out every few seconds, was forked like a serpent's. In the depths of his beady eyes, I saw the fires of Hell.

His massive chest was naked, but covered in thick hair. His hands had three sections with long dagger claws. His lower half was also covered in hair and ended in cloven hooves. He reeked of sulfur and death, and before I could react, he reached out with one hand and grabbed me around the neck.

In the next, the cavern disappeared. As he choked off my air and crushed my windpipe, the landscape around us changed until we were in an apocalyptic setting.

Ash fell from the sky, which was black and filled with clouds. What appeared to have once been a city had been reduced to rubble, shattered glass, and twisted metal.

Dead bodies and skulls littered the ground, and those beings still alive were missing parts—jaws, limbs, organs—as they crawled across the remains of buildings and roads.

Fires dotted the area, thick smoke rising in the distance. The only light came from those flames, and the temperature seared my skin as if I stood too close to one of them.

The monster lifted me off my feet and brought me nose-to-nose with him. His breath reeked of roadkill and sewer as he growled, "Welcome to Hell, *alciscor*."

CHAPTER TWENTY-ONE

When fighting an upper-level demon—*an original*—courage and balls are only going to get you so far.

Most likely, they'll get you dead.

"Master," I spat out, lowering my eyes as any good submissive demon should. My voice was barely a whisper. "It's an honor to finally meet you." Every word was like spitting out a piece of gravel. "Lilith told me so much...about you."

His tongue darted out and licked my cheek. I swallowed my revulsion. He then shook me so hard my teeth rattled. Grunts and words in that ancient language I didn't know came pouring out of his mouth, his snake tongue making weird loops and flicks.

Evil magic poured over me, and my demon clawed at her cage. I wasn't sure if she was trying to run away or fight him, but neither was a good idea.

He dropped me, and I collapsed on the ground, sucking in air and rubbing my injured windpipe. His disgusting feet were far too close to my face, but I groveled anyway. I needed to get my bearings before I took him and his magic on. I had no idea exactly how powerful he was, and I was out of my element.

Yeah, I'm a demon, but I've never actually been inside Hell's gates. Go figure.

Wings sprouted from his back. They were black, like Lucifer's, and yet completely different. While the fallen angel's were lush and glittered like obsidian, Ba'al Zebub's were thin, membranous, and bat-like. They snapped out, and I could see holes and tears in them, yet he didn't seem to care. His voice rumbled in perfect English, "Bring me the archdemon."

Damon. My breathing was ragged in the smoke- and ash-filled air, my larynx damaged, but it was the thought of giving him up that made my voice hoarse. "What...do you... want with him?"

Wrong question. The wings flared, and so did his nostrils. He kicked my shoulder with a hoof, sending me sprawling.

I slammed into a half-dead man with a missing eye and both legs. He moaned and tried to latch onto me.

Stomach lurching, I knocked him aside and jumped to my feet. I touched my ring fingers and thumbs together to activate my magic, relieved when it kicked in. A bubble formed around me, and I skirted the pile of zombie-like folks who had the misfortune to end up here.

The master demon huffed. "*Aious.*"

I didn't know what that meant. "Who's that?"

He stomped the ground and roared. "*Aious!*"

I struggled to keep my balance as the ground shook and a

crack formed near my feet. I held up my hands in supplication. This was his world, not mine, and I still had no idea if I could find a way out of it. "I don't understand the word. Tell me what it means."

The wings snapped in irritation. He raised a giant hand and pointed his claws skyward. Lightning forked from his fingers into the gloom above us, illuminating the smoky sky. Then he shot another bolt of power into a nearby heap of metal and wood, igniting it on fire.

A fireball punched into the air, and I flinched back. The dead and dying snapped back to life, fully intact. No missing limbs or visible wounds. They lined up like soldiers all around us, looking as shocked as I was at their sudden resurrection.

"*Aious*," he repeated, the word reverberating through my bones.

He could manipulate the weather, the ground, sling fire, and raise the dead—*aious*.

Power? Energy? Magic? All three?

He wanted Damon, not me. Why? What was it about my boss that this all-powerful being needed?

All-powerful. I stepped back, taking him in again. He was an Original demon. Was he one of the Omnis God had stolen from?

It still didn't answer why he wanted Damon...

Until it did. I nearly did a face-palm.

Damon wasn't an Omni—he was an *artifact*.

Ba'al Zebub's artifact, to be exact.

Lilith was now out of the picture, and Ba'al Zebub was giving the assignment to retrieve him to me.

Questions flooded my mind. If Ba'al Zebub knew

Damon embodied his missing power, why hadn't he gone after him and taken it back before now?

And how was I going to protect Damon from him?

All of that was whirling around in my mind. On top of that, why didn't he recognize the sliver of Omni power I commanded? Why wasn't he trying to rip it out of me for his own purposes?

God had stolen power from the three other Omnis. He'd created three artifacts to hold those powers. I'd assumed he'd done that because no one artifact could contain that much Omni power combined, but what if each Omni's essence was unique? Like fingerprints. DNA. They couldn't mix and match?

Before I could blink, Ba'al Zebub launched himself into the air. As he flew overhead, claws descended from his hooves, and he dipped down to grab me by the top of the head with one of his disgusting feet.

Sheer agony ripped through my skull as the claws dug deep. I screamed loud enough to shake the air around us. It was more than just a raw sound from my throat—it contained power that nearly matched his.

The split he'd started in the ground cracked wide open, swallowing some of his restored sufferers. The clouds above roiled, and lightning cracked between them.

My bubble of protection hadn't kept him from grabbing me, but now turned claw-like, matching his, and dug into his foot and ankle. The claws shredded through flesh and bone.

He roared and dropped me, and I fell at least a hundred yards until I landed in a heap of rotting corpses.

The shock of impact rattled my bones and nearly made

me black out when my head smacked into a skull. Hot, sticky blood poured down my face and over my ears.

My demon surged out of me hard and fast. The entire world around me went completely black, and my power flooded in all directions, becoming a torrent of destruction.

Once again, this level of Hell shook, but this time it was a tsunami. I couldn't see Ba'al Zebub, but his roar was cut short, and I heard him tumble through the air, his bat wings flapping like mad to try and keep him aloft.

My demon struck out with another wave of magic, and this time, there was a bright white light that came with it.

It slammed into everything. Every corpse, every skeleton, and every living creature. It banked the burning fires and obliterated the heaps of metal and glass.

I tried to rein her in, but there was no stopping her. A part of me didn't want to. It felt good to unleash her. To welcome my full powers.

My injuries mended themselves, and power lifted me to my feet. My ears rang, and my limbs were shaky, but I planted myself and drew up as much as I could from my surroundings.

The light faded. The world returned to its normal gloom. I glanced around and saw no trace of the previous destruction or bodies, but the ground was splintered into a hundred crevices and ravines.

There was no sign of Ba'al Zebub—only a vast, empty nothingness.

I sent a mental message to Lucifer, Damon, and anyone else who might have some dominion here and could assist with my escape. As I walked toward a distant light on the horizon, a giant serpent uncoiled from a ravine and reared fifty feet into the air.

Its maw opened, and it hissed, its forked tongue all too familiar as its beady eyes locked on me. I swore under my breath and glanced around for any type of hiding place. There was none.

My demon sent a surge of her magic into my bubble. As the serpent dove for me, I jumped over crevices and zigzagged my way across the open ground.

The fangs snapped inches away, my bubble repelling them but shuddering under each hit. Magic that scraped at mine tried to peel layers off it, the fangs seeking purchase. I fell, rolled, dodged—running but unable to get ahead with the ravines hemming me in.

I couldn't keep this up. I had to stop and fight.

But how? I'd never taken on a giant snake before.

It lashed me with its tail, lifting me into the air. I landed on the edge of one of the splits, hands clawing at the rim to keep from falling. As I chanced a glance down, I saw nothing but a black hole. A void of nothingness.

The soil crumbled under my fingers, and I slipped. I closed my eyes, reached for the Omni power, and attempted to catapult myself up.

It didn't work.

The beast struck the ground once, twice, three times, creating an earthquake of epic proportions. The ground broke free.

I dropped.

Screaming, I commanded my demon to save me. A flash of pure, raw magic exploded out of me again.

But it wasn't from my demon.

Wings erupted from my back, tearing through bone, tissue, and skin. My shriek was lost in the sound of their sudden flapping.

And then I was soaring up, up, up. I blinked, the feeling filling me like nothing I'd ever felt. I laughed, giddy with the sensation. As a demon, my magic was tied to the earth. Flying, as in an airplane, had never been comfortable.

But this? This was...dare I say it...heavenly.

And then I collided with a brick wall.

The impact sent me tumbling through the air. I had no control of my new wings, and the ground came up far too quickly. I tried to slow my descent, to right myself, but it was to no avail.

Bracing, I shut my eyes, the air streaming around my face, blowing back my hair...

Impact didn't come.

Instead, strong angelic mojo wrapped around my middle and yanked me up.

Opening my eyes, I found Michael hugging me to him. His blue eyes were a vivid neon, flames dancing behind the irises. "Silver, huh?" he said, making a clucking noise. "I thought for sure your wings would be gold."

I peeked left then right, seeing my wings were indeed a lustrous, metallic silver.

"It's the shade of the chalice," he said, before we swooped down over the serpent. "*The* chalice."

My breath caught, not only at the rollercoaster ride he was giving me, but at the sight below. The serpent was coiled and ready to strike—not at us, though.

Rad stood, feet planted, with Michael's sword raised above his head. His chaos demon had emerged, long, flying hair blowing on a nonexistent wind. His skin gleamed, his muscles rippling, and his face...that handsome face now resembled a Greek god, chisled from alabaster. The blue flames of the blade whipped around him in a swirling mass of fire.

He was beautiful, regal, and...

About to die.

For me.

"How is he wielding the sword?" I yelled.

"He has your essence inside him." This was said as if I were dense. "It's enough for the sword to recognize."

I shoved Michael away, my own wings kicking in as I aimed for the giant head of the serpent. It opened its mouth, about to clamp down on Rad and the sword, when I collided with it.

This impact was as brutal as the last one, and I bit my tongue. My ribs cracked, and I scrambled for purchase as I tried to steer as we swung back and forth. It tried to shake me off, but I held on for dear life.

It bellowed. I wrapped my wings around its eyes. "Get him out of here," I yelled at Michael.

Rad's eyes blazed with his demon energy. He sprang forward, jabbing the serpent's chest and slicing down its belly. "He's the serpent from the garden of Eden," Rad yelled at me. "Not Lucifer."

I was hanging on for dear life as the thing tried to buck me off. Rad's words didn't compute. Michael only added to my confusion when he yelled, "You can't kill it."

I summoned every bit of magic I could muster. "The hell I can't!"

"Kali!"

I looked down to see Rad tossing me the silver dagger he'd used on Lilith. Pure silver. A demon killer. "Stab him in the eyes!"

I had to release my hold with one hand to catch it, and that cost me. I was able to snatch the dagger out of the air, but I lost my grip, and that allowed the serpent to see out of that eye again. It shook its massive head with renewed violence, and I fell.

This time, it wasn't Michael who caught me. The serpent's giant maw chomped on me midair, one fang piercing my heart and the other my pelvis.

Between one heartbeat and the next, my body seized, my wings crumpled, and my magic winked out like a candle flame being extinguished.

The serpent gave another shake of its head, like a dog with a toy. Blood gushed from my wounds, and white-hot agony flooded through me.

Venom.

My limbs refused to move. My brain slowed. My breathing became ragged, and I couldn't swallow as my throat closed up.

I barreled down into the depths of my soul, searching for my demon, for the angel mojo, for *anything*, but I was hollowed out. Whatever venom the serpent possessed, it had neutralized it all.

It tossed me into the air and caught me again, the fangs sinking deep into my throat and my belly this time. I heard Rad yell and rage, and the sound of Michael's wings beating against the serpent's scales, but it all became a distant buzz in my head.

I couldn't keep my eyes open, and I had to keep blinking

myself awake, darkness threatening to take me under as my body caved.

When the serpent let me fall to the ground, I felt nothing upon hitting it. I lay close to one of the giant, jagged ravines and smelled the sulfur rising from it. Even that seemed flat, suppressed. The buzzing in my ears grew louder, my eyelids heavier. My wings vanished, and I tried to look at Rad, who was screaming my name.

Black dots swam in front of my eyes. My chest had a huge gap in it, the blood pouring out and soaking my clothes, my arms, and the ground. I tried to call to him. Tried to tell him I loved him.

All that emerged was a gurgling noise, accompanied by more blood.

A tug filled my entire body, and I glanced toward that light on the horizon. It seemed to be calling to me. Everything here was far away, remote, but that light seemed to glow brighter, stronger.

And then, someone was kneeling in front of me. Not Rad. Not Michael.

Highly polished black shoes and the legs of designer black pants flashed in front of me. "Do not die, Kali."

Damon.

No! He had to leave!

Get out of here, I yelled at him telepathically.

His magic coated me with a thick blanket of power, and I coughed up more blood. "Go..." I grunted. "You can't...be...here..."

The last breath left my torn lungs, and death took me.

CHAPTER TWENTY-TWO

Antiseptic tickled my nose, pulling me from nothingness. A low hum and a steady—if irritating—rhythmic beeping filled my ears.

A cavern loomed in my mind, right behind intense pressure in my eyes and forehead. As my awareness pulled itself out of the void-like cavern, my body woke in spurts. My mouth felt dry and cottony; my throat burned. My chest couldn't quite seem to expand all the way. Everything ached, as if it were on fire.

I managed to pry open an eyelid, then both, and found the world around me was blurry until I blinked multiple times. Each blink brought more into focus.

The bed I was in, the IV pumping medicine into my veins, and a person with tousled blond hair, a three-day beard, and wearing a wrinkled T-shirt and jeans, slouched in a nearby chair, sleeping.

The Institute's clinic looked exactly as it had when Rad had been the one on this gurney, but I saw it from a new angle. Lifting my head sent pain exploding along my spine and erupting from my lower belly. It spread in tsunami-like waves.

Gasping, I plopped back down on the pillow. I swallowed and blinked away the tears that instantly tried to leak from my eyes. What the hell? I'm not a crier, even when I'm in agony.

"Kali?" Having heard my gasp, Rad bolted out of the chair so fast he sent it skidding backward. He hovered over me, placing one hand on my arm and the other on the railing. "You're safe. Do you know who I am?"

I frowned. "Of...course...I do." The words were ragged, sounding as if I'd been yelling for days. "Why wouldn't I?"

Relief swamped his expression. "Thank the fires of Hell. I was afraid you'd come back..." He trailed off, looked away. He patted my arm. "I'll get Kirill."

I grabbed his wrist before he could move. "What... happened?"

He bent forward and kissed my forehead. "I've got to let Kirill and Damon know you're awake. Then I'll tell you everything."

Damon. His final words floated through my mind. *Do not die, Kali.*

Memories came storming back as Rad turned away. He grabbed the landline on the wall and poked at buttons as I grappled with the images banging around in my brain. Ba'al Zebub, Lilith, the pentagram.

The serpent. My body locked up.

Rad's voice was low but excited as he spread the word to the others. Lifting the covers, I glanced down to see I was naked under them, but bound in wide bandages that wrapped my entire torso. That's why I couldn't take a deep breath.

A fresh wave of agony ripped through me at the memory of the serpent's teeth clamping down on me. Twice. The way death had come in a rush, cold and black as sin.

Death. Had I actually died? *I was afraid you'd come back...*

Come back? I let the covers fall. Everything felt odd, surreal.

Rad appeared next to the bed again, smiling. "They're on their way."

"How long have I been...out?"

The smile fell. "Three days. We weren't sure you'd return at all."

Return? "Was I...dead?"

A grim nod of his head. "Ba'al Zebub killed you."

I rubbed the spot between my breasts, stopping to feel my heartbeat. It seemed weak, but maybe that was to be expected. I had no idea. I'd never died before.

Rad brushed a hair from my face. "Do you remember anything?"

"About the fight," I croaked, "or...dying?"

"Either. Both."

I drew in as deep of a breath as I could. "I remember you demoned-out. You wielded Michael's sword."

The corner of his mouth quirked. "Not on my bucket list, but it was pretty cool."

"I remember the serpent." I shook my head and ran a hand over my face. "I knew I was dying, and then Damon showed up. After that, there's...nothing."

I reached inward for my demon. Was she okay? Only a hollow void answered.

I frowned, my hand trailing to the right of my heart where I usually felt her. Closing my eyes, I drilled down deep, searching for my magic.

There wasn't any response

Panicked, I tried again.

Nothing.

"Rad?" My voice shook. "Where's my magic?"

He took my hand, kissed my knuckles. "It's not there?"

I shook my head. His form blurred, and my stomach heaved from the motion. I swallowed down the nausea and blinked a few times until his three heads became one again. My voice came out as a scared whisper. "I can't feel it."

His grip tightened. "It may take time for it to resurface."

The doors to the infirmary burst open, and Kirill raced in. He immediately checked my pulse, pupils, and the blood pressure cuff on my arm. "Your temperature is lower than your usual baseline, and your pulse is higher. Both are to be expected after what you went through. Otherwise, your vital signs appear within normal limits."

"To be expected after being dead?" I asked.

He pocketed his penlight. "Resurrection is outside my area of expertise, so that's my educated guess."

I felt weak and helpless without my magic. "What about my demon? When will she...come back?"

He froze for a heartbeat, then stared at the monitor beeping its irritating rhythm. "Your demon?"

"She's not..." I pointed at my chest. "Here."

He gaped at the spot I pointed to. Behind his eyes, I saw him processing that information. He cleared his throat and messed with the penlight. "No idea. What the serpent did... what Damon did..." He shook his head. "Well, it defies the laws of nature."

"Wait. You're saying—"

The archdemon in question entered, his woodsmoke hitting me at the same time his telepathy did. *Be glad you're alive.*

Lucky me—Damon's ability to enter my mind without invitation hadn't changed.

I tried to slam down my mental wards. They weren't there. *Fuck.* "You're an..."

He stopped beside the bed and glared down at me. "No, I'm not." He glanced at Rad and Kirill. "Leave us."

"Bossy as always," I muttered. I didn't want Rad to leave. "Rad stays."

Damon glared at me. "*Demanding* as always." When Rad raised a questioning brow, he conceded, with a brusque nod. "You may stay."

Rad resumed his seat. Damon propped a hip on the mattress, forcing me to ease over.

"You disappoint me," he said with zero preamble in regard to my health.

"Right back at you."

He quirked a dark brow. "I snatched you from death's cold, merciless fingers. How is it you're disappointed about that?"

How much did he know? I waved it off. "Thank you for resurrecting me, I guess. Where's my demon?"

"You *guess*? I can put you back in the grave, Kali."

"No." Rad jumped up from the chair. "She's just cranky. Cut her some slack. She did face off with Ba'al Zebub."

I glanced between them. "Is he dead?"

Damon's eyes were hard. "No."

Damn it. "Since when are you a necromancer?"

"My power gives me many abilities."

I fought not to roll my eyes. "And yet, you never mentioned that one to me."

"And you never mentioned several important things to me, either."

By the glower in his eyes, I knew the gig was up. Time to face the elephant in the room. "How long have you known?"

"About your betrayal—or the fact that you were carrying an essence inside you you couldn't control?"

"*Betrayal?*" I tried to sit up, hissed at the pain, and paused to steady my breathing. Rad reached out to help me, and I batted his hand away. Once I could speak past the agony, I glared at Damon. "I was protecting everyone."

His face was stern. "From *me?*" An accusation.

Thoughts tumbled through my brain. "Who told you?"

"Sal," Rad volunteered. "The moment you recruited him to research the Omnis, he ran right to Damon."

Of course, he had. Talk about betrayal. "I never should have trusted him."

Damon folded his arms over his chest. "He demonstrated more common sense than you have. Really, Kali. I never thought you'd be so easily manipulated."

My hackles rose. I wanted to shove him off the bed. "No one manipulated me."

"The angels fed you unconfirmed information, and you ran with it."

"I faced off with an Omni and consumed a piece of it. That was my confirmation they exist. Beyond that, yes, I listened to the angels because they were the only ones who had any idea about what that thing was."

"You should have come to me." The edge in his voice slipped. His expression turned sad. Hurt laced his tone. "After our past together, you chose to believe them and not turn to me with your suspicions."

I couldn't handle the disappointment in his voice. In his eyes. "You may not be an Omni, but you're an artifact. If you knew, you could have mentioned that to me in the past three centuries."

He sighed and ran a hand over his face. "I assure you, I am *not* an artifact. If you had simply talked to me, I could have told you so."

"Then why was Ba'al Zebub after you?"

"That's not your concern."

I eased up higher on the pillow, grimacing against the resulting pain. Rad handed me a cup of water, and I took a moment to suck it down. "I won't apologize for doing what I thought was best for everyone—demons, angels, and humans. I had no way to prove you *weren't* an Omni, and if you had been, I couldn't tip you off that I knew—or that I was hunting the artifacts."

He shook his head, dismay screaming through our connection and making my head pound more. "The angels have corrupted your thinking, and now you've appointed yourself omniscient."

"No, no, no." I handed the cup back to Rad. Frustration burned in my chest and throat. Emotions I wasn't used to played roller derby inside me. "The logic was sound. You fit the parameters. And it's a serious situation." I gave him the complete Omni For Dummies info dump, including that Michael had reported that the souls in Heaven were gone. How we assumed the Omnis were eating them as fuel. "You have to understand—until I knew for sure, I couldn't take the risk that you weren't one of these...*things*. You would have done the same in my situation."

He was silent for a long moment, considering my reasoning. "How do we know you aren't one?"

Another wave of emotion hit. This one was filled with skepticism and curiosity. But these weren't mine. They were...his? I shoved that thought away. "Me? An Omni?" I laughed, but it hurt, so I stopped.

His obsidian eyes flashed, and I felt a probe digging around my mind. "You claim to have a piece of one inside you."

I searched for that void, careful not to stoke the sensations storming through me—his, mine, even Rad's. They were different threads, all tangled up in my chest. But the abyss of the void seemed to be missing.

Relief tinged with regret filled me. Shutting my eyes, I tried to summon some angel mojo, remembering how it had felt to have wings. A tiny shred of peace sparked inside me, but there was no foundation for it. It was only a memory, not a connection to anything concrete. "It's all gone—my demon, whatever angel essence I had, even that shred of Omni power. Vanished. Destroyed. Obliterated?" I shook my head, feeling like I was drowning, the pounding in my head making the world blur again. "I've got nothing. I *am* nothing."

"You're human." Lucifer appeared behind Damon, dressed to the nines in a midnight-blue suit and tie. "Which makes you a target for every supernatural who wants the great Kali Sweet dead."

Damon stiffened, arms still folded. "Kali is no longer your concern."

Lucifer kept his gaze pinned on me. "The serpent consumed your magic. While Damon resurrected your body, your magic is gone forever."

Forever? It was a gut punch. "Can't you bring my demon back?"

Damon stood and pivoted to look at Lucifer. "I said, Kali is no longer your concern. Leave."

Satan's balls, here we go again. "Damon—"

"I was never the serpent," Lucifer told me. "It was always Ba'al Zebub. He tempted Lilith, then Eve. He knew they would succumb. I now realize he's an Omni. They couldn't have resisted his invitation to defy God even if they'd wanted to."

"And is he...gone?"

"We don't know," Lucifer and Damon said in unison. They glared at each other.

"So we didn't destroy the Omni, and I lost my magic." Not even Lilith's demise could make up for those two facts. "There has to be something you can do to—"

Black wings exploded from Damon's back, and his already tall, impressive body grew another foot, expanding enough that he Hulked out and tore his clothing. The shredded pieces fell from his muscled shoulders, leaving his powerful back and those glistening wings on full display.

The overhead lights gleamed off his tanned skin, from his chest down to his thighs, as the wings rippled in anger. He was in full archdemon mode —and he was magnificent.

Rad and I exchanged a glance, Rad shifting closer. A breeze blew against my skin, his chaos rising.

If only I could smell it.

Damon's next words came out in a snarl. *"Get out."*

Lucifer's jaw tightened. Rad tensed, flinging out a hand. I suspected his magic had formed a bubble of protection around me, but I could neither see nor sense it.

Damon's wings fluttered as the two males faced off. Another dungeon repeat was brewing—only this time, I had no means to stop it.

Lucifer shifted to the side so he could meet my eyes. "There is nothing any of us can do. I wish you well." He gave a mocking bow and vanished.

Pressure built inside my skull and pressed hard against the back of my eyes. Human. *I'm human.*

No wonder these emotions were causing havoc with me. That my body was in such pain. Before I could snuff it out, a whimper hiccuped free.

Rad instantly turned, lowering to the mattress to gently pull me into his arms. "Shh. It's okay. We'll figure it out."

I sobbed into his shoulder. I tried to drag in his scent, but there was nothing but a soap and laundry detergent fragrence. That hit me harder than the fact I was lying in a hospital bed feeling helpless.

"I've lost...my magic." I couldn't wrap my head around it. "My demon is gone."

He stroked my back. "It'll be an adjustment, but we'll take it one day at a time."

Damon's voice cut in. "You'll stay here."

I lifted my head from Rad's shoulder to see he'd returned

to his normal size. The wings were gone. He'd used his magic to repair his clothes as if he'd never torn them apart.

I scrubbed the stupid wetness off my face and shook my head. "Clearly, I've crossed a line with you that I wish I could uncross, but I can't. I'm not staying where I'm not wanted. "

He narrowed his eyes, and more of that hurt passed over his face. A sensation that echoed it hit me square in the chest. Hurt, disappointment, guilt. "You *are* wanted, Kali. More than you know."

CHAPTER TWENTY-THREE

After forty-eight hours in the infirmary, I was climbing the walls. Rad fussed and doted on me. Di read me stories and offered to give me a makeover. *Hard pass*, although I did look like hell.

Maddy stuck me in a wheelchair, took me to the media center, and forced me to binge-watch her favorite movie franchise.

Even Faron and Bane stopped by to check on me when picking up assignments from Damon. The two of them had been helping out during my absence, which appeared to be permanent.

"Taking on an Omni without me." Bane tsked. "Next time, you'd better let me in on the fun."

"If Ba'al Zebub is still out there," I told him, "you'll get your chance."

The weirdest and most complicated of my visitors was Damon. He barely spoke to me, although he brought me books on philosophy and poetry. He also dumped off stacks of files on demons and other supernatural beings who were causing problems in Chicagoland. They were ones I'd normally be assigned to. I couldn't hunt them down, but Damon wanted my insight on them anyway.

Typically, I would've ignored all of the reading and focused only on the files, but there was something different between Damon and me now. One thread had been broken, but a new connection that went beyond what we'd had before had sprung up.

This went beyond our telepathy and was wholly emotional. It was overwhelming to sense everything he was feeling on top of what I was feeling as a fledgling human. When I broached the topic to see if the connection ran both ways, he claimed it didn't.

And I instantly knew he was lying.

Mostly, he continued to project continuing anger, disappointment, and a certain level of sadness. Underneath all of that, I picked up on other feelings. A desire to protect me, to shield me, to return me to the demon I had been, but a helplessness because he couldn't.

Because of all of that, I found myself poring through the books he brought. Granted, I didn't understand most of what the philosophers wrote, but it was almost as if their words and ideas matched Damon's. I could imagine him writing the texts and even the poems himself.

I hadn't spent much time with Neve over the past few months, but she made it a point to stop by several times a day. We discussed what it meant to be human.

While she was somewhat unusual with her ability to talk

to spirits, she did a good job reminding me of why I loved humans. She talked about the soul and bucket lists. Even told me how excited she was to explore the meaning of life with me.

Go Team Human.

I hadn't realized how difficult it was for them. Sure, I'd seen them struggle, but those struggles paled in comparison to constantly dealing with Heaven and Hell, angels and demons, fighting the apocalypse, etc. After spending time with her, I was reminded of the amazing ideas humans have produced, the complex emotions they deal with on a daily basis, and their never-ending curiosity, innovation, and creativity.

Their ability to adapt and innovate had proven to make them the most successful of any species, supernaturals included, on the planet. There was a piece of the Omni they referred to as God in each and every one of them.

Given her penchant to see and speak to spirits, she'd taken a few lessons from Keisha on summoning and directing them. She was full of curiosity.

Nearing midnight on my third day stuck in bed, I was feeling a bit innovative myself. I decided to make a break for it.

Rad was working, and neither Kirill nor Sera was in the infirmary. I unhooked myself from all of the equipment, but swayed on my feet when I stood. My slowly healing wounds rebelled, the skin on my abdomen going tight at the move- ment. I clutched at my belly, and it took a minute for the lightheadedness to pass, but once it had, I wrapped a jacket that Rad had left behind around me and headed for the door.

Taking the elevator was risky, since the Institute was always busier at night. Demons preferred the graveyard shift.

I made it to the stairs and halfway to the next floor before my legs were trembling so hard I had to sit. I hated being so weak and felt overwhelming impatience at the slow healing. This being-human gig wasn't for the faint of heart.

Lainie found me still stuck on the steps sometime later. I expected the house mother to escort me back to my hospital bed, but she squeezed my shoulder and managed to get me to the elevator and to my former apartment upstairs without anyone being the wiser.

Rad had taken over the small suite, and his clothes, guitars, and random sheets of music were scattered amongst his weapons. Exhausted from the simple exertion of walking, I thanked Lanie and sent her on her way so I could crash.

This bed was much more comfortable, and it smelled like Rad. I nestled in and was asleep in minutes, and didn't wake up until light was streaming through the window.

He leaned over, kissing my forehead. "Good morning." There was a tray on the bedside table with coffee, bagels and cream cheese, and a bowl of fruit. "Lanie sent this up for you. She said she'll bring a protein shake in an hour. You need to build up your strength."

Kirill and Sera were unhappy that I'd ditched them, but over the next several days, my recovery sped up. I ate better, got more sleep, and started tackling the stairs twice a day. At first, I could barely make it up and down one set. By day five, I was climbing to the top level, barely winded.

Between protein shakes and stair climbing, I dug out my father's writings and went to the Institute archives. I researched Ba'al Zebub and Omnis.

I found myself in the company of Sal, and more than once, he offered to show me some of his research. I wanted to reject it and tell him off out of spite, but I didn't. Any information I could glean about my subjects was important, and his research skills were superior to mine. He also brought me coffee and small treats from the kitchen—cookies, brownies, even Pop-Tarts, which I had a new craving for.

This was his way of trying to befriend me again, and I accepted every treat, even though my waistline was starting to grow uncomfortable. I didn't, however, give him any indication that we were friends. He had a purpose in my plan for now, and I wouldn't forgive him for his betrayal.

One afternoon, he brought Shayne with him. Both of them looked like kids on Christmas morning. Before they even reached the giant mahogany library table I was seated at, I said, "What is it?"

"Jedidiah," Shayne said as they stopped on the other side. He looked like he'd just discovered the cure for cancer. "Shlomoh. Better known as King Solomon."

I knew little of the Biblical king. "What about him?"

Sal leaned forward, placing his hands on the tabletop. "The Ark of the Covenant—it's an artifact."

"One of my earliest incarnations was as an advisor to the king," Shayne cut in, his Aussie accent strong. "Most of what's written about him is only a fraction of the truth. His temple, his library, his treasures... It's all been vastly under-reported."

The Ark was said to house the original Ten Commandments, sure, but... "Why do you think the Ark is an artifact?"

"Because of something he said to me while I was in his court.

He told me God had come to him in a dream and given him a 'spirit' to place inside it. In a dream state, he was led to open it, and he told me the spirit that went into it was a *black void*."

My grip tightened on my pen. "You're only remembering this now?"

He spread his hands wide. "Crikey, old mate, it's been three thousand years. I've forgotten more than I remember. It was only when I was reading one of Sal's lost books that a story jogged my noggin."

"See,"—Sal pulled out a chair and sat—"there are two Arks: one on Earth and one in Heaven."

My father's writings had mentioned the same idea. That the items within the earthly Ark—the manna, Aaron's rod, and the Ten Commandments—all symbolized Jesus. The Heavenly version symbolized a risen Christ and a new covenant with his followers. "And?"

"I believe they're directly tied together. That's the reason no one has found the earthly version—it's hiding more than what the records claim."

A piece of one of the Omnis. I tossed down the pen and sat back. "I don't suppose you know where we can find the Ark?"

Shayne's grin widened, perfect white teeth flashing against his tan skin. "No, but I bet Damon does."

I tilted my head. "Why?"

"Another thing that's been stewing around up here." He circled a finger at his temple. "Solomon conjured angels and demons to do his bidding. One of his favorites was an archdemon named Lock. Lock escaped Solomon right before the King's reign began to crumble. Some said Lock's disappearance caused King Solomon to fail. Damon has changed faces and names, but I think he's Lock."

"You *think*?" I needed proof. "That's not good enough." Especially not after my previous assumption had been so wrong.

Shayne paced the length of the table and doubled back. "Ba'al Zebub was also a favorite of Solomon's, only he always kept him contained with Lock's help inside the conjure circle. Lock, however, could be trusted, according to the king, and he was free to roam the temples and compounds. The two of them worked hand in hand, but Ba'al Zebub swore vengeance on both the last time he was brought forth. Shortly after that, Lock disappeared, and Solomon became ill and frail."

Had Damon been walking the earth for three thousand years? "That's still not enough." I glanced at Sal. "Why don't you simply ask Damon if he's Lock?"

He reared back. "Me?"

I gestured at the stacks of books, parchments, and notebooks. "Nothing in any of these texts suggests an Omni or a Damon connection to Solomon or his treasures, so the only thing we have is Shayne's somewhat faulty memory. Since we're now assuming that Damon himself is *not* an Omni, what does it hurt for you to ask him if that's why Ba'al Zebub was after him?"

The two males exchanged a glance, and in it I saw the truth: they were afraid Damon might kick them out if they revealed they knew his true identity.

"Oh, I get it. You're afraid of him— so throw me under the bus and let me eat the consequences."

"You're his darling," Sal said with a sneer in his voice. "He won't throw you out. You can do no wrong."

I came out of my chair and leaned on the desk to get in his face. "I've never been his darling. I've been a tool for him to use to hunt down rogue demons, and I was damn good at that job. But now? I'm nothing. I betrayed him, and you were the one who informed him of that betrayal. My sanctuary here is iffy at best. You're the sainted historian. You're the one who's uncovered this theory. March yourself to his office and present it to him."

The two of them left, but I doubted that's where they were going.

I made notes on my paper, doodling in the margins. This was at least a new angle to look at, and I really had nothing to lose. The next time I had a chance to talk to Damon, I would just point-blank ask him.

I finished off my third protein shake of the day, closed the notebook, and headed to the apartment to change clothes. It was time for my daily workout with Cole.

Out of all of my friends, he knew me best—and he was the only one who didn't coddle me. He'd visited once while I was still in the infirmary, told me to knock off the pity party about being human, gave me exercises, and told me to meet him in the training center at four pm prompt today.

To say I was a little nervous was an understatement. In the apartment, I changed into workout clothes, hid the notebook under the mattress, and grabbed a bottle of water. Rad was between jobs, but was on his way to the next.

We exchanged a few comments, a long embrace, and a deep kiss. At least, he was fully recovered from his entanglement with the *lecura*, and his chaos was under control. He hadn't had any more episodes, and I knew that he felt a good deal of pride and satisfaction at having taken out Lilith.

Things between us had been somewhat normal, but strained. I tried to act like my old self, but I could tell he was worried about me, even though I was recovering. Sex had changed. I could no longer handle the extremes I had before, and my current lack of stamina made it that much harder. My previous libido had been high. Now, it was almost nonexistent. As I grew stronger, I hoped it would come back.

Cole was sparring with one of his soldiers, stripped down to his pants, his chest gleaming with sweat as the two of them punched and kicked and traded insults.

Spotting me, he broke off and sent the soldier to the showers, stripping off his gloves as he looked me over from head to toe. "You've gained a few pounds and have color in your face again. Looks like you're improving." He grabbed a towel hanging on one of the ropes and wiped off his face, the back of his neck, and his chest. "Have you been doing the exercises I gave you?"

I called up my best confident swagger and strode to a nearby bench, setting down the water. "Twice a day, every day."

When I turned back to him, he crooked two fingers at me. "Get in the ring."

I started to balk, shut my mouth, and did as told. I needed to get back into fighting shape.

After an hour of him chasing me around the ring and beating the crap out of me, I held up my hands in surrender. "I need a break."

He snorted. "Your enemies aren't going to give you a

timeout because you're tired, Kali. Hands up, tuck your elbows. Plant your feet."

I did all three things and landed on my ass, anyway. After a few more disastrous tries, he gave up. He stripped off my gloves and tossed them aside, handing me a fresh towel. "What have I always taught you about taking on an enemy who's bigger and stronger than you are?"

I was gasping for breath, and everything from my throat down to my hip bones hurt. I took the towel and began wiping the sweat from my face, neck, and arms. "Leverage." I gasped. "We use whatever we can to level the playing field."

"And how do we do that?"

"I used to do it with magic."

He whacked me on the side of the head.

"Ow! What did you do that for?"

He backed me into the corner of the ring, placing his hands on the ropes on either side to pin me in. "I've taught you the art of war. I've taught you strategy. I've taught you how to use weapons and your brain to amplify your natural fighting abilities and crush your enemies. None of that has changed because you don't have magic."

He was right. I knew hand-to-hand, how to use a sword, a dagger, throwing stars, and more. I knew how to suss out my enemies' weaknesses and use them to get the upper hand. Most importantly, I had always known what my strengths were and I'd played to them. "I can't fight supernaturals using nothing but strategy and weapons."

He boxed the side of my head again. I yelped and covered my ringing ear. "Bullshit. You can, and you will. I won't let you die on my watch."

My irritation turned into full-blown anger. I shoved him

backward, surprising both of us. "I'm doing my best, dammit. Back the hell off and leave me alone."

He grinned. "Now, we're getting somewhere." He hitched a thumb over his shoulder. "Three laps around the gym. Go."

The idea of running made me want to collapse, but I was annoyed enough to do it anyway. I wouldn't give him the satisfaction of complaining or failing.

I started fairly strong, but by the first turn, I was already sucking wind. I slowed my pace, so I was barely moving faster than a walk, and by the time I'd made one full lap, I thought I was going to pass out.

I took a water break, noticed him glaring at me, and slowly returned to the track. Before I knew it, Maddy was there, dressed in spandex, with her long hair pulled into a high ponytail. She fell into step beside me, keeping her pace as slow as mine, and acting like this was normal.

"What are you doing?" I asked between great inhales. I sounded like I had emphysema.

She didn't miss a beat. "I've taken up running. Thought you might like the company."

"Since when are you a runner?"

I didn't miss the quick flick of her eyes toward Cole. "Last week...?"

It sounded more like a question than an answer. "Liar. What did he do to coerce you into this?"

"Nothing. I want to help," she said under her breath. "I honestly hate running, but if it motivates you, I'll run to the North Pole and back."

My throat closed up. I pretended to wipe sweat out of my eyes, but it might've been something else. "I'm not your queen anymore, you know." I knew the rules, and it was bad enough that I've been a demon who stepped into the role, but a human had no chance of being accepted by the vamps. "You don't have to brown nose me."

She gave my arm a playful punch. "Don't be an idiot. You're my friend."

The next to show up was Dru, in loose-fitting shorts and a Bulls t-shirt. He joined us, falling in on the other side of me. "What a perfect day for a run."

"I appreciate the support, but you don't have to do this," I told him.

He didn't look at me, but he did smile like a kid with a secret. "Why wouldn't I want to jog with two lovely ladies?"

Maddy made gagging noises. I shook my head. "So you two are going to show up every day when I work out to keep me motivated?"

"If that's what it takes," the master vampire said. "We need to get you back into shape. Shouldn't take more than a few weeks. Or..."

When he didn't continue, I knew something was up. "Or what?"

"There is a way for you to regain supernatural powers." This time, he glanced at me, his smile turning cunning. "All you have to do is say the word."

I didn't have to contemplate the meaning of that. I'd already considered it. I'd also already discarded the idea. "I don't want to be a vampire. Start looking for a new queen."

"All I ask is that you keep your options open. Being turned isn't a walk in the park, but the rewards are worth it."

"And you'd be my sire, which means I'd be tied to you for my immortal life."

"You make it sound as if that's a fate worse than death."

In some ways, it was. "Learning to be human is an adjustment, but I'm going to make it."

"Of course you are," Maddy said. "You're still Kali Sweet."

Dru's smile vanished. "I can't keep the lid on this much longer. You're due to come to the House at the full moon, as per normal, but the moment you step inside, every vampire in the place will know you're no longer a demon. I can make an excuse for you to miss this month, but after that..."

We'd completed another lap. Maybe having running buddies wasn't so bad. "I know—the word will get out, and that's when all of my enemies will come for my head."

Next to show up were Faron and Bane. I'd completed my three laps and now dragged myself to the bench where I sucked down the last of my water and stretched out, limbs trembling. The two vampires continued their campaign to get me to reconsider Dru's offer to turn me. They made good points, but the only reason I didn't argue was that I was too tired to form sentences.

The Fate and her bodyguard grabbed staffs from the weapons wall and began sparring. Neither said a word to me, and I wondered if they were actually there just to work out.

But then Di and Neve showed up. The two spoke to Cole in hushed voices, and then he called me over. Maddy and Dru followed, and Faron and Bane stopped sparring, walking over to the group as if they wanted to hear what Cole had to say.

The War demon reached for me. "Give me your hand."

I slid both behind my back. Sweat trickled down the side of my neck and into my collar. "What are you doing?"

Cole held out his hand, palm up. "What did I say about leverage? About leveling the playing field when you're at a disadvantage?"

"That I need to outthink my enemy, use a weapon to amplify my skills, play my strengths and their weaknesses...?"

"Give me your hand, Kali. I'm about to give you leverage."

Dru held up a finger. "*We* are about to give you leverage."

I was pretty sure I wasn't going to like this, but I trusted Cole more than anyone outside of Rad. Tentatively, I placed my hand in his.

He withdrew a short dagger with an antique handle from his pants pocket, and when I tried to jerk my hand away, he locked his fingers around my wrist. "Stop it."

I jerked harder. "No. What are you doing?"

Neve began chanting under her breath, and quicker than I could blink, Cole drew the tip of the blade across my palm, producing a gash that oozed blood. Then he did the same to his palm, before slapping it into mine, mixing our bloods.

A shot of heat lanced into my hand and up my arm. He handed the blade to Dru, who cut his palm and then handed the blade to Maddy. Around the circle it went until everyone was standing in line, ready to share their blood.

"This is a bad idea," I said as Dru took my hand next.

Master vampire power surged into my body. "It's only a tiny bit from each of us, because your current form can't handle too much, but this will give you an edge, all be it temporary."

As Neve's chant grew louder, I tried to talk each of them

out of it, even Di. She held my bloodied hand tenderly and hugged me as her goddess power slid into my system. "I wish I could give you so much more."

As she pulled away, her magic sealed the cut. My entire system buzzed with all the different magics. My ears rang, my vision blurred, and my stomach cramped.

But oh, the high followed was pure bliss. I closed my eyes, letting it sweep me away. It seemed like eons since I'd felt this sensation.

A pop and flutter of wings alerted me to another visitor. "You started without me."

Michael. I opened my eyes to see him towering over everyone and frowning. He jutted his hand toward Cole and the dagger. "I offer myself as tribute."

Maddy gave me a regretful look. "I should have never let him watch Hunger Games."

"I don't want your blood," I told him.

"But it can help you," he countered.

"If you want to help me, let me keep the sword."

"Humans can't wield it."

I showed him my bloody palm. "For a little while, I'm more than human."

"What's your plan?" Bane asked. "We donate some blood every few days?"

I looked to Cole, then Dru. "The supernaturals who want revenge are going to catch up with me eventually. I say we go on the offensive."

Cole smiled. "Sounds like you're strategizing."

I smiled back. It was something I'd been thinking about for days. "I'm going to need a small army. Does anyone want to volunteer?"

Maddy's hand shot up. Michael mimicked her. Di wiggle her fingers at me, and Neve said, "I learned a lot from Keisha and Amy. I'll work on some spells."

Faron and Bane exchanged a look. She shrugged. "Sure, why not? Things are slow in the destiny world right now."

Cole slapped me on the back, which nearly sent me sprawling. "Let's meet at seven tonight to discuss this plan."

I left the gym feeling stronger than I had in days.

CHAPTER TWENTY-FOUR

The cocktail of magics did funny things to my system. Hot flashes, then chills. My head felt like it was going to explode; then it would be filled with dozens of ideas.

I stumbled like a drunk at times, only to turn around a minute later and glide like a ballerina.

The best part, however, was connecting with Volante. While the whip was now just camouflage for Michael's sword, it still carried all the attributes of my faithful weapon. There was no demon left in me to command it, but the fresh magic swirling in my veins still acted as a conduit.

Inside the apartment, I played with her endlessly, switching her between whip and sword to re-familiarize myself with both.

Kirill hunted me down and chastised me, but we both knew the truth—he was relieved to be rid of me.

Rad returned at sundown and found me in bed. "You look...better," he said, flicking his gaze over me in a long perusal. "Almost like you're old self."

I'd found one of my short skirts, a black lace top that showed off my midriff, and I'd painted my nails black. I'd left my hair down, but applied eyeliner and mascara. I greeted him with a long, demanding kiss before stroking Volante, who was wrapped around my arm like normal. "I am better."

He wrinkled his nose. "You smell...weird."

"Di gave me a basket of bath care products—roses and jasmine. You know how she is with her romance intentions."

He cocked his head sideways. "It doesn't cover up the War demon and vampire stink."

"About that." I wrapped my arms around his neck. "I have a couple of things to tell you."

Over the next few minutes, I explained what had happened and my plan going forward. I can't say he was exactly excited about any of it, but he helped me work out a few details.

He was going to miss the seven o'clock meeting—Damon had a loose succubus that needed shutting down—so I promised to bring him up to speed as soon as he returned. I needed to get a few things in place before I left the Institute, anyway, and that meant I'd be spending another night here.

At seven, my posse arrived, Maddy with snacks, Dru with wine. My plan was simple and took ten minutes to share. Cole punched holes in it. We brainstormed, and by nine, we had two backup plans along with the main one.

For the first time in days, I felt like myself.

I was too cued up to go to bed, so I wandered the archives. I reread passages of my father's work, imagining my mother, the Oracle, as she channeled the stories to him. My chest ached with guilt and grief over their absence. I missed my little sister, too.

There's little about the Ark of the Covenant in the biblical version of Revelation, but in my father's text, I found two paragraphs on it.

According to him, it played a key role, along with the Tree of Life and the Tree of the Knowledge of Good and Evil, in melding Eden with the future home of God and his followers, the Holy City.

Three symbols, two present in the Christian origin story.

Adam, Lilith, Eve, the apple, the serpent...my mind spun up a hundred theories. Adding in King Solomon and his treasures, there were plenty of potential artifacts. I wanted to talk to Lucifer, who'd also played a part in the world's origins, but he wasn't returning my calls.

Fatigue crept up on me. The last time I glanced at the clock, it was nearing two a.m. I planned to read one more passage and crash—then woke in a strange bed with an even stranger bedfellow.

The body I was curled around was warm and hard. My limbs felt heavy, my eyelids refusing to open. My mouth was dry again, but I was too relaxed to get up for water. I trailed fingers over Rad's chest, wondering how I'd ended up in bed when my last conscious thought was about the Tree of Life. He must have found me there asleep and carried me upstairs.

As my fingers roamed, he sucked in a sharp breath and hissed. The scent of wood smoke teased my nostrils, and I heard Damon's voice in my head. *Kali?*

Lethargy left in a rush of shock. My eyes flew open and I shot upright—staring down at my boss. "By the fires of Hell," I said. "What are you doing in my bed?"

His hair was tousled, his chest bare. "You're in *my* bed."

"What the fuck?" I glanced around, realizing he was right.

We were in a huge four-poster bed draped in black-and-red silk. Dark wood furniture and an ornate vintage fireplace created a living area off to the right.

Heat flushed my cheeks. I scrambled backward, tangled in sheets, and landed on my ass.

I jumped up and glanced at my clothes. My shirt and skirt were gone. I was in my bra and panties. "What the fuck?" I repeated again, whirling around to find my clothes.

"You were sleepwalking," he said. His voice was low and rough, and there was a lot going on under the sheet from the way it was tented. I'd felt his repressed sexual frustration around me before, and it was a storm right now, battering into me, even though I sensed him trying to suppress it. "I tried to wake you when you crawled into bed, but couldn't. I'm not sure why. Did you take a sleeping pill?"

Once, when I'd been under extreme stress, I'd done some sleepwalking. I'd come to his room to lead him to the dungeons, but I hadn't ended up in his bed.

My shirt was on the floor a few feet away. I snatched it up and pulled it on. "I've never taken a sleeping pill in my life."

"Some cause sleepwalking in humans."

"So you just let me crawl into bed with you?"

"As I said, I tried, but there is scientific evidence that states it's best not to wake a sleep—"

"Never mind." I cut him off as I ran to my discarded skirt near the door. "What time was that?"

He hadn't moved, remaining flat on his back as if he feared he'd scare me off. "Around two. You came in, stripped, and climbed under the sheet. You were out like a light. When I attempted to leave, you latched onto my arm and wouldn't let go."

I glanced at his bedside clock. Three hours ago.

I tugged on the skirt and combed my fingers through my hair. Embarrassment was eating me alive, but I chalked it up to an aftereffect of the weird blend of magics in my blood. "I'm sorry. Obviously, I didn't intend to barge in here and..." I gestured at the bed, my gaze landing on his very healthy morning erection. *Gah!* "I didn't do anything else, um, inappropriate, did I?"

He propped himself up onto one elbow, the faintest twitch of his lips holding back a smile. "No. You slept deeply. Another reason I was reluctant to disturb you. I know you haven't been sleeping well."

He should've woken me. He should *not* have let me lie there nearly naked in his bed. "I'll get out of here. Again, I apologize. I don't know what happened. And let's never speak of this again."

His lips did that quirk again. "I'll see you in my office at eight."

I raced to the door, throwing a wave over my shoulder. "Be there with bells on."

I sprinted to my apartment, shut the door, and leaned against it, blowing out a huge breath.

Thankfully, Rad had been out all night on the hunt. My chest hurt thinking about trying to explain this to him.

Better to forget it ever happened, right? There was no need to upset him over a stupid sleepwalking incident.

But...how was I going to look Damon in the eye at eight when we had our normal morning meeting?

More importantly, how was I going to keep this from ever happening again? Was this something my new human self was going to do on the regular?

I was still leaning with my back against the door when the handle rattled. Someone pushed from the other side, and I stumbled forward.

"Kali?" Rad stood in the doorway, frowning. His tired gaze scanned my attire and tangled hair. "You just getting in, too?"

I pressed a hand against my skirt and tried to look like that was exactly what had happened. "I fell asleep in the archives."

He shrugged off his trenchcoat and hung it on the hook next to the door. "How about a shower and a nap?"

I pasted on a smile. "Sounds wonderful. I'll start the shower."

In the bathroom, I stripped and blasted the hot water. Guilt nudged. I should tell him what had happened, and by not doing so, it felt like cheating.

Ridiculous, that. Of course, I hadn't. I had no control over what had happened, and yet, I was very reluctant to share it with him.

A few minutes later, his hands under the warm water made me forget about everything except him.

CHAPTER TWENTY-FIVE

At eight on the dot, I pressed a hand on my nervous stomach and knocked on Damon's door.

It opened on its own. Across the room at his desk, he gestured me in. He was dressed in a dark gray suit, crisp white shirt, and silk tie. His hair was slicked back, and he hadn't shaved, a shadow of whiskers covering his jaw and upper lip.

I wasn't exactly full of energy after a couple of rounds with Rad, but I was feeling better and still buzzing from the orgasms. For this meeting, I'd gone with black pants, a red shirt, and sensible boots.

I crossed the room and set a stack of papers on his desk. "My research and analysis of the activity happening in Hyde Park." He'd given the assignment to Rad, but I'd jumped on it. "You have a gang on your hands. Rad's going to need one of Cole's Merc teams in order to round them up. The gang itself is a mix of several tiers of demons, a shifter, a djinn, and an unknown—possibly the succubus you have Rad chasing. They're all connected, and they strike every three weeks."

Damon barely glanced at the papers. "You're not going back to the church."

I paused. "What?"

"We've discussed this. You can no longer defend yourself against supernaturals, hence you're staying here."

How had he found out about my plan? I hated it when he was always a step ahead of me. "Look, I appreciate the resurrection, which I've stated more than once, but I can't live here until I die." Which was going to happen sooner than I'd like. The mirror had just shown me how much faster I was aging. "I have to learn to live in the real world again. I'm not without skills or brains."

"You have work here. You have purpose."

"Research isn't a purpose, Damon. You're babysitting me. I have a business to run and things to do. I'm going home."

He tossed down his pen and glanced up. Fire lit his eyes. "You're a fool."

It was rare for Damon to use that term. I'd betrayed him and had been wrong about many things, but it still hurt that he didn't have more faith in me.

I eased into one of his visitor chairs. How many times had I sat here under his tutelage, under his scrutiny? Looked like it was time to use some of the skills and brains I'd just touted. "Tell me about King Solomon and his treasures."

Now it was his turn to pause at the change in direction. "Why?"

I kicked my feet up on the corner of the desk, going for casual. "You didn't recognize Shayne when he showed up?"

He studied me for a long, slow heartbeat. "Are you feeling all right?"

"Deflect all you want, but I know you were part of Solomon's court back in the day. An archdemon that he relied on to become one of Israel's wealthiest and wisest kings."

His brow furrowed at the same time his lips quirked. Not like they had earlier that morning at my embarrassment, but in bewilderment. "Another wild angelic speculation?"

I knew it was a façade. "Stop blaming the angels for everything. They believed what they told me about you being an Omni, and I believed it, too. What's done is done. There's no going back. We move on." *I move on.* "This is about you and Ba'al Zebub. I need to know why he's after you so I can protect you."

He leaned back in his seat and let the smile break free. This time it was in pure amusement. "You're going to protect me?"

"Stop patronizing me. Even if I don't have my demon anymore, I was reminded yesterday that I'm really good at outsmarting other supernaturals. I'm the best you've got for strategizing ways to sabotage them. You may have escaped his claws for all this time, but he got close to you, and it nearly cost me very dearly. It's personal, now, for me. So pony up the truth. We've always worked well together. I want to get back to that."

Kicking his own feet up on the corner of his desk, he steepled his fingers. "Working together requires trust. You obviously don't trust me."

I'd never seen him put his feet on his desk or appear so casual, but there we sat, both of us pretending to be blasé and unconcerned about the outcome of this conversation while we glared at each other across his desk.

His emotions were somewhat muted today. I wondered if he was purposely putting up a shield to keep me from reading them. What did slip through was lighter. There was something that seemed like affection, hope, and curiosity. There was also a thread of tolerance for my disrespectful pose.

This connection between us still freaked me out, and I wondered whether it would last. If so, I would need to figure out a way to suppress it myself. I didn't want to be aware of his thoughts and feelings.

I mimicked his steepled fingers. "Ba'al Zebub wants vengeance. That's a subject I'm an expert in. He and Lilith nearly killed Rad, and he did kill me. You may be content to sit back and avoid him. I'm not. I want revenge."

That made a muscle in his jaw twitch. For all his casual demeanor, I was getting under his skin. "You couldn't handle him at full power with Michael's sword."

I held up a finger. "But I wasn't prepared. He came out of nowhere. Part of the art of war is knowing your enemy. I've been doing a lot of research on him. He won't take me by surprise again. But books and written accounts aren't the same as someone who has firsthand knowledge." I gave him a pointed look. "Help me—or when I die, you'll live with the guilt that you didn't."

He heaved a dramatic sigh. "You're out of your league."

"Why did you take me under your wing after I destroyed Queen Maria?"

He studied my face as if looking for deception. "Because I knew you had potential."

"Plenty of supernaturals had potential, Damon. Why me?"

"I assure you, it was not because I'm an Omni and grooming you to find my artifact."

I didn't appreciate the sarcasm in his voice, but I let it slide. "That doesn't answer my question."

His focus dropped to the stack of papers, although I sensed he was seeing something else. "Ba'al Zebub is my brother."

My mouth fell open. "You're joking."

That rogue smile ghosted across his lips again. "If only I were."

"You and..." I whistled softly. "Wow. Hard time wrapping my mind around that."

"In the demon world, bloodlines and alliances are...odd. Unlike humans, we don't necessarily have physical parents. He and I were created at the same time, both of us in line to take the throne of Hell. That is, until God forced Lucifer on us, and the entire hierarchy changed."

"You sold out Ba'al Zebub to King Solomon."

"I never wanted to rule Hell like he did. I wanted Earth. Solomon offered me a way to walk here, and my brother was no angel, as they say. You witnessed that."

"If he wanted to rule Hell, why did he care if you wanted Earth?"

"Why indeed?" He studied his fingers. "I never understood it. I removed myself from Hell, which would have made the path to the throne easier—if he could overthrow Lucifer."

There was the rub. "He figured that out, didn't he? He

was never going to overthrow a fallen angel, and so Earth was his next conquest. Except, you were already here."

He shrugged. "It doesn't matter if you're human, demon, or angel—you always want more. Even if he'd become ruler of the Pit, he would've wanted the Earth."

I picked at a thread on my pants. "And here you sit, three thousand years later, and you haven't taken over. If that's your goal, you need a new plan."

He chuckled. "I've lived an extraordinary life. The adventures I've had, the people I've met, the women I've loved. The things I've experienced..." He gave an awestruck shake of his head. "When Solomon released my bindings, he taught me a great lesson. Being a ruler comes with its own kind of chains. To be truly wealthy and powerful, one needs freedom."

Sounded logical to me. I tended to be a one-woman island, not liking to rely on others, and certainly not wanting to feel responsible for them. Over the past few years, that had changed, and now I was glad for my friends.

But there was no way I'd ever want to rule over anyone. I certainly didn't want to take over the Earth. The only reason I'd bartered with Lucifer and Michael about becoming the ruler of Hell was to save my friends if Paradise was restored on Earth, kicking all demons to the Pit. I didn't crave power the way most demons did. I craved justice.

"Thank you for sharing that with me."

His eyes flicked to mine, then away. "The only way to handle my brother is to keep him in Hell. He is a terror and is able to shapeshift into almost any form, making him difficult to defeat. Rad is lucky it was Lilith using him and not Ba'al Zebub.

If he takes over your body, you die. But I fear that the necromancer learned too much from Lilith about opening that portal. I've had Faron and Bane hunting him, but he's disappeared."

"Did they destroy the pentagram?"

He gave a brief nod. "But if Tromble Lope still knows how to re-create it..."

"We need to shut him down."

"Neve has used her pendulum to search the maps for him, but nothing has emerged. She's spoken to spirits, but that hasn't produced results either."

"What do you want me to do?"

He raised a skeptical brow." I want you to stay inside the Institute where you'll be safe."

"Because you're my friend and you're worried about my health, or because you still have plans for me?"

The brow rose even higher. "Can it not be both?"

"Sure, but that's not what I want to hear." I dropped my feet and stood. "I have enormous respect for you, and I've been your tool for a long time, Damon. I signed up for the job, knowing that you were going to use me to accomplish what you wanted for the Bridge Institute, and sometimes for your own personal desires, but I thought, after all this time, maybe I meant more than that to you."

He heaved another of those deep sighs, as if I were testing his patience. That wasn't uncommon. "I've asked great things of you because you have the potential to change the world. You've already saved it multiple times. You've held some of the greatest power that has ever existed in your hands, and instead of using it for your own gain, you used it to save those you love. You're motivated by love, an uncommon emotion for a demon."

All of that was true. Yet, I yearned for him to say he just wanted to be my friend. "I'm still going after your brother."

"Stay here for now, and I'll tell you everything I know about him."

It was tempting, but I had something to deal with first, before the magics in my system drained away. "He's not the only one I'm going on the offense with. I'm going to the Chicago House to resign as queen."

"How many blood types did you ingest?"

He'd figured that out, too. "A few. The vampires won't be able to tell I've lost my demon yet. This is my chance to walk through the midst of them, resign, and no one be the wiser. Once that's done, I've got a list of top enemies most likely to come after me once they hear I'm human. My team and I are going after them first."

"Your team?"

I nodded. "I'll have round-the-clock bodyguards for forty-eight hours. I plan to make that time count."

"And then, you'll return here and allow me to educate you about Ba'al Zebub?"

"If you promise to help me kick his ass."

Damon rose and extended a hand. "It would be my pleasure."

I shook it, tried not to lose myself in his dark eyes, and headed for the door. Just as I grabbed the handle, he said, "Kali?"

I glanced back.

"Our friendship is more important to me than the Institute. Don't forget that."

CHAPTER TWENTY-SIX

The following morning, I watched the sun rise from my favorite spot on the church rooftop.

It felt good to be home, although after the recent events, it also felt strange. I wasn't the same person. Not the same demon.

My midnight announcement at the Chicago House drew mixed reviews. Most seemed relieved that I was resigning my post, since none of them loved demons. A few questioned my story about the Bridge Institute eliminating my position and investigating one of my recent cases. Without their backing, I explained, I was on my own.

Through some creative research, Dru also dug up a couple of outdated rules in the vampire canons that said my role as queen of the Central United States had to be reverted since the Bridge Council was investigating me for misconduct. It was time for him to find my replacement.

While at Carpathia, I'd also let it 'slip' that I was closing Sweet Investigations. Without the Bridge's backup and support, I couldn't run my business of serving justice to supernaturals.

Vampires are bigger gossipers than humans. Within hours, it was all over Chicago that I was on my own—no Bridge Council, no vampire house—and that I might end up in the Institute's dungeons.

Dru helped further by leaking the story about his fight with Rad to his vamps, telling them how even the former rockstar had abandoned me because of my involvement with angels.

Even though my demon was gone, my pride was still intact. This was a farce to a large extent, but I still hated it. As if I would ever do anything that would cause the Institute to kick me out and investigate my methods.

In some ways, however, that's exactly what Damon had done. He'd known almost from the beginning that I was secretly trying to prove he was an Omni, and yet, instead of confronting me, he'd attempted to get me to confess. When I hadn't, he'd locked me out.

It was another thing, in a long line of incidents, that kept me walking on eggshells with him. Was that how friends treated each other?

I sipped my espresso and noticed movement a hundred yards on the other side of the cemetery. Remaining unconcerned, I thought about Damon. Hearing about his past plans and what he'd chosen when it came to power gave me a fresh respect for him.

The being moving toward the church was likely one of my top ten. As the breeze shifted, the cold air brought the scent of Noctifector. The demon-hunting group had been around since the Middle Ages, maybe longer, and they were all human. I'd been on their most wanted list for a long time, but they'd left me alone once I rescued Rad from their clutches and kidnapped one of their most prized hunters, Parker.

The Noctifector wouldn't be alone. They always traveled in packs. I stood and stretched, acting like I didn't have a clue he and his buddies were surrounding my place, while I listened to Cole and several of his soldiers fire off updates in my ear comm. We'd already disposed of six of my top ten, and their bodies were stacked like icicles in one dark corner of the graveyard.

We let the Nocts get into the yard before they were taken out in a simultaneous assault that was nearly as quiet as the frigid dawn.

Once daylight was in full swing, time ticked by slowly. By noon, we'd had no more visitors, and I assumed it would stay that way until nightfall. Supernatural assassins tended to prefer the cover of darkness.

Still, I found I couldn't sleep. It could've been too many espressos, but my mind kept circling the same problem. Once my borrowed magic ran out, what was I going to do as a human?

I could keep being an investigator, but I couldn't take on supernatural clients anymore. I could keep working for the Institute like Damon wanted, researching and analyzing the continuous flow of creatures that preyed on humans, but what did I really want to do?

I wanted to keep helping humans. That had been my purpose for a long time, and just because I was one now, didn't mean I wanted to stop. The only question was, what was the best way to do it?

A knock sounded, and Cole grumbled in my ear. "It's Brianna and Vicky. You don't have to talk to them if you don't want to. I can handle it."

I could guess why Vicky was here, but what did Bri want? I tapped the earbud. "I'll talk to them."

Brianna was Dru's right-hand lieutenant. She was also his blood bag. They had a rather intimate relationship, and she'd never liked me.

At one time, she and Cole had carried on a sordid affair, even though he hated vampires with a passion. She was perfectly pretty in that vampire way, but her personality wasn't as lovely. "This is a surprise," I said when I opened the door, wedging my body in it, so they knew they weren't welcome to enter. "What do you want?"

Bri's hands went to her hips, and she scanned me from head to toe. "What's going on? And don't give me that bullshit about the Bridge Institute tossing you."

She was too smart for her own good. "I don't know what you mean? My life is shit right now, Bri. Go away."

When I started to shut the door, she shoved a hand against it and pushed. Even with the magics in my system, her vampire strength was more than I could handle. I stumbled back.

She breezed into the foyer, disgust twisting her face as she sniffed me. "I knew it. I knew you smelled different. Where's your demon?"

Vicky nodded, narrowing her eyes at me as she followed her in. "Told you."

Dammit. "She's been suppressed. Damon sequestered her until the investigation is over. Not that it's any of your business."

Bri snorted. "Sequestered your demon? Yeah, right. Like that's a thing."

I thought it sounded good. "What do you care? You should be thrilled that I'm no longer queen."

She crossed her arms and cocked a hip. "Oh, I am. More than thrilled. But I need to know—whatever is going on with you isn't going to blow back on Alexandru, is it? This excuse you gave is covering up something. I don't need to know what it is, I just need to know that my master is safe."

She took her role as his second-in-command seriously and guarded him like a hawk. I couldn't blame her for wanting to make sure he'd be okay. "There won't be any blowback on him." I held up a hand like I was swearing on a Bible. "You have my word."

She studied me for a long moment. "That's what he said, too, but I wanted to hear it from you. Are you in some kind of trouble?"

"You have no idea. Now, if that's all...?" I gestured at the door. "I'm a little busy. Oh, and Vicky?" I mimicked writing a check. "Lilith is dead. The rest of your payment is due for services rendered."

She shot daggers at me. "Your boyfriend killed her, and since he's an employee of the Institute, your payment is forfeit."

She had me there. It was a technicality, but true. I hate her even more for that.

Bri stopped at the door. "Every supernatural in the city is going to be coming for your head, you know."

"Yes, I'm well aware. That would be the reason I'm busy."

"I don't care what happens to you, but you mean a lot to

him. I don't want him upset. I know Cole and some others are watching your house, but if you need another set of eyes —or a kill squad—you come to me, got it?"

Touching. Cole was rattling off a bunch of crap in my ear. I tapped the comm unit to silence him. "That's generous of you, considering our backstory. I assure you, I'm in good hands."

She reached into her jacket and pulled out a plastic bag. Inside were gray and white ashes. "I already took care of three vampires planning to stake and then burn you. You can thank me later."

She tossed the baggie at me and walked out, throwing the door open and leaving it that way. Vicky didn't bother to glance back as she followed.

I hustled to the opening and called out, "I owe you one."

Both of them flipped me the bird over their respective shoulders and kept going.

I tossed the vampire remains in the fireplace and turned it on. Rad wasn't due back for another hour. He and one of Cole's teams were chasing down the gang I'd told Damon about. He hated leaving me, but that was our life now. I had to be able to handle things on my own. This round-the-clock babysitting could only go on for so long.

I headed upstairs and soaked in the tub for a few minutes. Having not slept since my accidental venture into Damon's bed, I yawned and sank back against the clawfoot tub's high porcelain back. My body ached, and I traced a finger over my healing scars. They would never fully go away, but the mix of magics was helping.

When the last ounce of heat bled from the bath, I forced myself out and dried off. A few minutes later, I climbed under the covers, intending to take a short nap before Rad arrived.

Sleep hit hard and fast. The next thing I knew, night had slipped into the room, putting it in thick shadows.

The nap left me feeling worse. My limbs felt like brick weights. My head was groggy. I sat up, brushing back my hair to check the clock.

That's when I saw Damon sitting in a chair across from me.

"Damon? What are you doing here?" A thought struck, and I sat up straighter, swinging my legs around. "Where's Rad? Is he okay?"

He tilted his head, dark eyes glittering. A string of ancient words flowed from his mouth and sent chills raking down my spine like barbs.

I knew that voice, and it didn't belong to my boss.

I'd removed the comm unit when I'd bathed. It was still on the bathroom sink. I eased over on the mattress, working my way to the opposite side. I had weapons in the nightstand and under the bed. All I needed to do was get to them. "You're not Damon."

A deep chuckle made the hair on the back of my neck stand at attention. "No, *alciscor*. My brother is dead."

Dead. Damon. My heart squeezed.

Ba'al Zebub stood slowly, eyeing Damon's form before his malice-filled eyes zeroed in on me again. "You and I have unfinished business."

I dove for the floor, reaching under the bed—only to be yanked away from my weapons and hauled up by my hair.

Screaming, I dug deep for whatever magics might still be in my system...and came up empty.

He held me face-to-face, my feet dangling inches off the floor. His rancid breath shoved its way up my nose. Even though my scalp shrieked at the rough treatment, I used feet and fists to pummel him, causing my body to twist back and forth.

He shook me like a rag doll, and some of my hair tore free, causing me to cry out again. He tossed me onto the mattress, a gravely laugh coming from his mouth. "Did you think I wouldn't come for you?"

How had he gotten topside again? The pentagram? Who'd summoned him?

Whoever it was, they were the reason Damon was dead.

And they were now at the top of my kill list.

I scrambled backward, falling off on the other side of the bed this time. No sense wasting energy replying. I only had one chance to escape this. One chance before he grabbed hold of me again and ripped me to shreds.

Volante hung on the wall near the closet. I clambered to my feet and ran for her.

Ba'al Zebub caught me before I got halfway there. His hands morphed into claws. He sank them into my arms before slamming me against the wall, barely missing an eye with one of the wall hooks. "You'll be my pet in Hell for all eternity."

Never! Whatever I had to do, I was not going anywhere with him.

Breathing through the pain—so much worse as a human—I called on Cole's training. Ba'al Zebub, even in Damon's form, was at least seven inches taller than me and outweighed me by sixty pounds.

And he'd killed Damon.

The rage that filled me was a blessing. I stopped registering the pain, the smell of him, any fear. He was going to do whatever he wanted with me, but I was going to put up a damn good fight before I let him.

He yanked me back and started to bang me into the wall again. Instinct took over, thanks to Cole's years of training, and I wedged my foot against it. The archdemon's force nearly broke my leg, but it threw him off his game. I brought up my other foot and used the wall to push as hard as I could.

He stumbled. It eased the pressure on my legs, and even though he didn't release me, I used my weight to drive him back even farther.

We fell to the ground. He grunted but didn't turn loose. I tried jamming my elbows into his face and body, but he had a hold of my arms, blood leaking all over from the injuries. I fought as hard as I could, using my feet to kick him and jerking my weight from side to side.

I tore one of my arms free, the claws ripping my flesh. Then I flung myself at Volante again, and this time, she responded. Her hilt flew into my outstretched hand, and I didn't waste a moment. In one fluid motion, I pivoted and snapped her toward his face.

As the tip of it lashed his cheek, she morphed, becoming the flaming sword.

The archdemon bellowed and shifted into his true form. The floor was slick from my blood; as I raised the sword and lunged, I slipped.

But the sword did its job. As I fell, I managed to slam the steel blade directly into Ba'al Zebub's heart.

Blue fire exploded. The archdemon grabbed the blade

and jerked it out of his chest. It flew from my hand and skittered across the floor.

Flames raced up my arm and into my heart. It stuttered. Ba'al Zebub gained his feet and wrenched me up.

In his soulless eyes, I saw the fires of Hell, and a cry of vengeance ripped out of me, shattering the windows and rattling the church's foundation.

One of his claws dug into my chest, grabbed my heart, and...

The church, the sword, and something inside me snapped together like puzzle pieces. A flashbang went off, and everything went white.

CHAPTER TWENTY-SEVEN

In the white void, sensations pummeled me—not emotions, but physical blows.

Entities swam in and out of me like fish through water, each one raking against my spine. Voices wailed in my head, a cacophony of words and screams.

"What's dead should stay dead," a deep bass voice spoke through the abyss, echoing off my bones and making my brain feel as if it were about to split open.

I clutched at my ears as if that would help, but the sound was inside my skull.

It didn't matter if I had my eyes open or closed; everything was pure white. A white so intense that it seemed to burn my corneas. A figure emerged from the light, cloaked in black robes and carrying a scythe.

Death.

I'd met the Horseman who traveled as Death, but this one was different. This was the Grim Reaper version. The one who came for humans.

Two glowing orbs appeared where eyes should have been, casting light onto his bony skull. The light reflected off the silver blade of his weapon and pierced my eyes.

I tried to back up, but I had no balance since there was no solid ground under my feet. It felt as though I were spinning, totally unconnected from anything, and I threw my arms out in an effort to try and right myself.

Damon had managed to cheat Death and resurrect me. Now, the reaper was coming for retribution.

Since I couldn't run, and I had no idea how to fight him, hopelessness rose like a wave inside me. The entities continued to batter me, knocking me around and increasing my instability.

Rage flamed hot inside me. I was sick and tired of all of this. Tired of being hunted. Tired of being attacked.

"Stop it!" My yell echoed as loud as Death's voice, and I felt the world around me shudder like it had in the church. "*Fermati!*" Enough. I'd had fucking enough.

The horribly bright light dimmed. The entities stopped. When I blinked, the world around me became a monochrome gray. The reaper cocked his head. His glowing eyes scanned me. With a jolt, I realized I'd sprouted wings.

I glanced over each shoulder, seeing the beautiful silver feathers fluttering with a violet aura. At my command, they beat ever so slightly against the air.

Death took a step back. "You are..."

An angel.

I shook my head. "I'm a demon with some confused DNA. Any chance you can reunite me with my demon self? She was taken from me, and I want her back."

His voice seemed to drop another octave. "You are an *abomination*."

Oh. Guess he wasn't impressed with the wings. My bad. "Maybe so, but it's impolite to shame people about their natures. I mean, you don't see me standing here calling out your horrifying ugliness, do you?"

Death reared back as if I'd slapped him. "This cannot stand."

My wings rippled, and a wave of pleasure went through me. "Yeah, well, take it up with your boss. I didn't ask for any of this, and until you have the balls to actually come after me with that blade? Do yourself a favor and stay out of my way. I'm done playing nice."

He seethed, and I felt it in my bones just like I had his voice.

But I wasn't backing down. "Send me back to Earth. Or to Hell. I'm fine with either. I have an archdemon to hunt down."

He cocked his head again, as though I were the oddest thing he'd ever encountered. Maybe I was. "You are not free to go anywhere."

He didn't seem to understand that I wouldn't tolerate his attitude. With my wings, I now found myself steady as a rock. I moved forward, not even needing to step. "Let me clear up your misconception. You're not in charge of me. You can't—"

He disappeared in a flash of light, leaving me all alone in this weird space between life and death.

"*Porca miseria*." I glanced around, tested out my wings a bit more, and then sighed. "Lucifer?" I called. "Michael? Anybody?"

My ears popped. A hard tug yanked at my chest—and then I was back on the floor of my bedroom, hands sticky with blood, broken glass everywhere, Damon's ashes in a macabre pile before me.

I no longer had wings, but I definitely felt different. A presence floated nearby, and a woman's voice with a thick southern accent said, "Oh dear. Whatever happened to the poor man?"

Slowly, I raised my gaze and saw a ghost staring down at the ashes that formed the outline of Damon's body. Her slim fingers created a sign of the cross over her chest. Her slippered feet didn't touch the blood or the shattered glass. Her gown was old-fashioned, and she had her hair in a braid, topped with a cotton nightcap.

Her eyes flicked to me, sad and curious at the same time.

"Who the hell are you?" I asked. It hadn't been unusual for me to see spirits when I'd still been a demon...

The thought hit so hard I nearly toppled over. Internally, I searched for her, and I felt the strangest spark inside my chest next to my heart. Just a tiny flicker of flame. Was it her?

"I'm Delilah," the ghost said. "I usually live out there." She pointed to the graveyard. "I felt a strange...pull. Something dragging me in here."

She looked me over, her eyes taking in the blood covering my torso, arms, and hands. Self-conscious, I stuck them behind my back and stood. I felt woozy, and my heart ached for Damon.

"He was trying to kill me." No sense trying to explain to her that he'd been possessed. "You probably should leave. Go back to the graveyard."

"But you can help me." She turned in the air, showing

me her back. There was a large kitchen knife shoved between her shoulder blades. Blood had leaked from the wound and stained her nightgown. "You need to find my killer. Make sure justice is done for me. Then I can move on to the other side. Go to heaven, where I belong."

A massacre had occurred on the cemetery's grounds. A massive-scale sacrifice that had been made. When I'd come across the church and grounds, I'd surmised it had been made to Death himself.

In the center of the graveyard was a portal to other worlds. Whoever had sacrificed so many souls there had opened that portal, and after purchasing the entire area, I'd done my damnedest to keep it sealed.

I suspected Miss Southern Belle had been one of the sacrifices. If her killer had been mortal, he or she would be dead themselves by now.

If they were supernatural, maybe I could get her justice —not just her, but the other ghosts still chained to the cemetery.

I shook my head. Ghost-whispering was Neve's department. I had bigger issues on my plate. "I can't guarantee anything, but I'll look into it, okay?"

She vanished, and I turned my attention back to the ashes. Was Ba'al Zebub truly gone? I went inward, searching for my new connection to Damon. "Come on. Please. Let me know if you're still there."

Nothing answered. Just overwhelming emptiness.

Grief and anger warred with each other inside my chest. If he'd just listened to me. If he'd taken more precautions.

What exactly would those have been? He'd said the pentagram had been destroyed. Had the necromancer created a new one? I slammed my hands on the floor, the impact enough to shake the pile of Damon's remains.

This wasn't my fault, and yet I was filled with guilt. I'd had my chance to eliminate Ba'al Zebub in Hell, and I'd blown it. I'd been so caught up in my own issues that I hadn't done enough to ensure the archdemon couldn't rise again and come after all of us.

But I was also angry at Damon. He'd withheld information until I'd point-blank put him on the spot. All of this could've been avoided to begin with if he'd simply confided in me.

Footsteps thundered up the stairs. "Kali!"

Rad and Cole burst into the room, pulling up short when they saw the destruction and me hunkered over what was left of Damon. "He's dead," I said, my voice breaking. "Ba'al Zebub possessed his body, and I..." I couldn't say it. I'd killed a primordial demon—and my boss.

My friend.

Rad grabbed my shoulders and pulled me away from the remains. "Thank the fires of Hell you're okay."

Cole kicked at Michael's sword. "The blade worked for you?"

Numb, I nodded. "I don't know why. All of the magics that you shared with me had run out. But something happened when he attacked. I fought, and I thought I would lose, until this weird..." How to describe it? "It was like the church and the sword bonded with each other, and together they connected with me."

The three of us frowned down at the blade. I explained what else had gone down, but then a sob tore out of my throat.

An emotional rockslide once again hit me. I was overcome with all that had happened to me in the past week.

Ever since my encounter with an Omni, my life had
been one long descent into weird. I'd gone to Hell. I'd
sprouted wings. I'd died and been resurrected.

I'd been one of the most powerful supernatural creatures
on earth, only to have it all stripped away.

And then, I'd met the Grim Reaper.

"Damon has survived worse," Rad reminded me. He, in
fact, had once decapitated Damon in order to kill Death the
Horseman, and I'd barely spoken to him for days afterward.

I shook my head. "Lucifer once told me that what was
done by Michael's sword can't be undone. Even if some part
of him was still in there,"—I pointed to the ashes—"I killed
him along with Ba'al Zebub."

"Killed who?" a familiar voice asked.

We all whirled to find Damon in the doorway.

With a cry, I threw myself at him. "Satan's balls, how are
you alive?"

His confusion swamped me. He peeled back from my
embrace to give me a questionable look. His brows knitted
and his mouth turned down in a disgusted frown as he took
in my appearance. "Why would I be dead?"

I turned so he could see the room. "That pile over there
is you."

As he moved to inspect the ashes, he was careful to step
around the larger pools of blood. He took everything in with
his dark eyes before they returned to meet mine. "Explain."

I was so happy I didn't register my own emotions rising
up like a tsunami. I repeated the story, watching his surprise
and a new emotion take root in his chest. Pride. At me.

His voice softened as his attention went to my neck. "You have done the extraordinary again."

Rad, standing next to me, touched the skin where Damon stared. "The scrolls are back."

Most of the time, the scrolling silver tendrils decorating the side of my neck and trailing over my shoulder were invisible. They looked like a tattoo, but were actually a type of bruise from Dru tapping directly into my carotid artery when I'd given him my blood to save his life once.

I clamped a hand to my neck, then rushed into the hall to look in the mirror. Rad and Damon followed. Sure enough, the scrolling lines flashed a bright silver.

The same shimmering shade as my wings.

My legs went weak. Rad grabbed my arms to keep me from falling. "What is it?" Rad asked. "What's wrong?"

Damon took my other arm, and they guided me to a nearby chair where I dropped onto the cushioned seat. Damon folded his arms and stared down at me, while Rad knelt beside me.

"I suspect your angel essence was never destroyed," Damon said. While you couldn't feel it or access it, it still resided inside of you. You broke through some barrier when you held the sword this time."

As if in response, his wood smoke scent wafted over me. The smell of Rad's demon, that blend of ocean breeze and salt, did as well. I blinked as both of their auras flickered into view, and a familiar heat bloomed in my chest.

I shot to my feet. "She's back."

The two males exchanged a look. "Your demon?" Rad asked cautiously.

The smile that broke across my face was so big it nearly hurt. I placed a hand on my chest. "I can feel her."

Touching my thumbs and ring fingers together, I brought up a bubble of protection. It burst out of me like a magical fire hose, knocking both of them off their feet and sending them skidding across the landing to the stairs.

Cole came running out of the bedroom. "What the fuck is going on out here?"

Not realizing it was there, he bounced into the bubble and flew backward as well. He landed in the bedroom doorway, shock on his face.

I threw my head back and laughed. My wings exploded out of me, and I felt the scroll tattoo light up icy cool.

It wasn't a bruise...it was tied to my angelic essence. When the master vampire had bitten me, it had activated whatever this was that had been suppressed in my DNA. As a *vitium*, I had chalked everything up to being both good and evil, but now it seemed even more true.

I pulled the bubble back, searched for my demon, and found her irritable. She swatted at my attention, wanting to nap. I let her. She'd been through as much as I had, and it might take a while before we were back on good terms with each other, but I welcomed the challenge.

I helped all three of the males stand, hugging each one and kissing them on the cheek, because my joy was too much to keep inside. I did a little dance on the landing, Rad grinning, Damon frowning, and Cole shaking his head and retreating back into the bedroom.

"Who wants coffee?" I called, nearly flying down the stairs to the kitchen. My magic was back, and it was more powerful than ever. I could feel it. I couldn't wait to let everyone know.

Lilith was dead. Ba'al Zebub was dead. Damon was alive. There were plenty of demons to hunt down and kick their ass back to Hell. There was still the problem of the Omnis, but we had a starting point—find the Ark of the Covenant—and Damon, who could help us track it down.

In the kitchen, Rad ground espresso beans while I heated up the machine. I gathered cups while he sorted through the pantry, pulling out lemon biscotti and my favorite chocolate spice cookies.

Only when I took a moment to glance out the kitchen window did I do a double-take.

"Ah, Rad?"

"Yeah, K?" He slid up beside me, following my pointed look. "What is it?"

"You don't see them?"

Damon and Cole entered the kitchen, Cole heading right for the espresso machine. "See who?"

Damon's magic engulfed me as he came up behind me to peer over my shoulder. "That's quite a gathering."

"Gathering of what?" Rad asked.

My stomach tightened. "He can't see them."

Cole now joined us, the four of us squeezed together as he, too, studied the graveyard beyond my back door. "I don't see anything but trees and grave markers."

"But you see them, right, Damon?"

"Yes, but I've never noticed so many gathered there before."

Impatient, Rad leaned closer to the glass. "What are you talking about?"

"Ghosts," I said softly. "Dozens and dozens of them."

Rad and Cole exchanged a look. "Is the portal open?" Cole asked, setting down his cup and reaching for his dagger.

I shook my head. "My wards are holding. This is...something else."

What's dead should stay dead. The words rang in my head. The creepy sensation of all of those entities swimming through me returned. I shuddered.

"Can you help me?" A tiny voice said from behind me.

I whirled, crashing into Damon. He righted me and turned as well, and we both stared at the ghost in the kitchen doorway.

She was no more than 14 or 15, but dressed in modern-day clothing. She wasn't from the graveyard; she was from somewhere else. A much more recent death.

I swallowed hard. "Help you with what?"

She held out both arms, revealing deep wounds carved into her wrists, blood painting her hands. "I'm not supposed to be here," she said. "I made a mistake, and he used me. I need your help so I can leave this place. Find him." Her face turned ugly, angry, and vengeful. "Make him suffer like he made me suffer."

I looked to Damon. His dark eyes glittered. "What's his name?"

"I don't know, but he was into black magic. Pentagrams and candles and raising demons."

"Guess who," I muttered. "Where did you meet him?".

"A club." She glanced away, as if embarrassed. "I had a fake ID that said I was twenty-one. My friends and I went there, and he was kind. Handsome." Her voice dropped to a whisper. "I was a fool. My parents don't know where my body is. If I take you there, will you tell them? Make sure he's caught?"

I heard Damon take a deep breath. He turned to me. "Looks like you have a new type of clientele to find justice for, Kali."

My demon woke, eager for the hunt. Behind us, Rad and Cole seemed to understand that we were talking to a spirit. Rad's hand landed on my lower back, comforting and supportive.

"What's your name?" I asked the ghost.

"Lindy. Lindy Collins."

I gestured for her to leave the doorway. "Let's go to my office. You can give me the details."

As she floated out of the way, I glanced into the living room and blinked. Dozens more hovered there, as if this were a waiting room.

Damon stepped up next to me. "You're going to be busy, but I expect you back at the Institute first thing tomorrow night. You've got a lot of work to do."

I stared at the ghosts, feeling both my angel and demon respond. "I'll be there. You can count on it."

Then I led my new ghostly client into my office and shut the door behind us.

KALI'S TAKING *on ghosts and more in the next installment in the Kali Sweet Urban Fantasy Series. Don't miss Sweet Underworld, releasing in 2026!*

· · ·

BEFORE YOU GO, **I've got a special FREE gift for you...**

Rad Beaumont's band, *The Chaos Demons*, just dropped their debut album — and you can get it **FREE** as a thank-you for reading *Sweet Betrayal*.

Use the exclusive coupon Chaos at <u>https://mistyevans books.com/product/kali-sweet-songs-for-the-damned</u> and step inside Kali's world like never before.

FREE URBAN FANTASY! GET REVENGE IS SWEET, KALI SWEET URBAN FANTASY FREE

Step into the thrilling world of the *Kali Sweet* series—a snarky, fast-paced urban fantasy adventure packed with vampires, shifters, demons, angels, and a fierce heroine you won't forget!

If you're a fan of paranormal books featuring strong female leads with razor-sharp wit, sizzling romance, and jaw-dropping twists, this series is for you.

Dive into a world where the supernatural collides with high-stakes drama. Kali Sweet isn't your typical heroine—she's a no-nonsense, supernatural-busting force to be reckoned with. Whether she's outsmarting vampires, taking down rogue shifters, or facing off against celestial beings, Kali's brand of snark and courage will have you hooked from page one.

Fans of urban fantasy series like *The Dresden Files*, *Mercy Thompson*, or *Kate Daniels* will love the Kali Sweet series. Watch now to experience the magic, humor, and danger that define this unforgettable paranormal universe.

Don't miss the chance to start your next favorite urban fantasy series. Click here to grab your FREE copy of Revenge Is Sweet today!

SONGS FOR THE DAMNED - CHAOS DEMONS ALBUM

Wanna raise a little hell?

I'm Rad Beaumont and I'm giving you a FREE gift!

Grab your free copy of *Songs for the Damned* — the debut album from my band, **The Chaos Demons**.

These tracks were written in blood, sweat, and heart-break (thanks, Kali).

Hit the link, crank the volume, and join the chaos.

Use your exclusive coupon Chaos at https://mistyevansbooks.com/product/kali-sweet-songs-for-the-damned **to get the full album FREE.**

Then keep reading for the story behind the music...

NEW ALBUM from The Chaos Demons — *Songs for the Damned*

They said demons can't love. They said salvation wasn't for us.

They were wrong.

Rad Beaumont and The Chaos Demons are back with their darkest, loudest, most soul-shattering record yet. *Songs for the Damned* is an 8-track descent into love, chaos, and rebellion — written in blood, sweat, and riffs.

From the haunting ballad *Whisper in the Dark* to the apocalyptic firestorm of *Eden Burns,* every track drips with the fury of Hell and the fragile hope of love. These are songs for outcasts, fighters, lovers, and anyone who's ever stared down the dark and dared it to blink first.

Because sometimes the damned have the best stories to tell.

🎶 Featured tracks include:

• *Blood & Stardust* — a vow written in fire and obsession.

• *Chains on Fire* — the sound of breaking free.

• *Human After All* — a tender anthem for the strongest woman he knows.

• *Forever Damned, Forever Yours* — the closing ballad that proves love survives even in Hell.

TURN IT UP. Break the chains. Burn the Garden.

For all the Kali Sweet fans, this is *Songs for the Damned.*

https://mistyevansbooks.com/product/kali-sweet-songs-for-the-damned

PNR & UF BY MISTY/NYX HALLIWELL

The Accidental Reaper Series, available in ebook, print, and audio

Grim & Bare It, Book 1

Reaper's Keepers, Book 2

In Too Reap, Book 3

Killin' It (short story for newsletter subscribers only)

The Vampire's Kiss (an exclusive short story available in Misty's Store. *Intended for mature audiences* 17+)

Grave Girl

Grave Magic

Grim Vows

Undead Ever After

To the Grave & Back (January 2026)

Listen to the series on the Eleven Reader Publishing App!

The Kali Sweet Series, available in ebook and print! Coming soon to audio.

Revenge Is Sweet, Kali Sweet Series, Book 1

Sweet Chaos, Kali Sweet Series, Book 2

Sweet Soldier, Kali Sweet Series, Book 3

Sweet Curse, Kali Sweet Series, Book 4

Sweet Malice, Kali Sweet Series, Book 5

Sweet Betrayal, Kali Sweet Series, Book 6

Listen to the series on the Eleven Reader Publishing App!

Witches Anonymous Step 1

Jingle Hells, WA Step 2

Wicked Souls, WA Step 3

Dark Moon Lilith, Witches Anonymous Step 4

Dancing With the Devil, Witches Anonymous Step 5

Devil's Due, Witches Anonymous Step 6

Dirty Deeds, Witches Anonymous Step 7

Wicked Wedding, Witches Anonymous Step 8

Listen to the series on the Eleven Reader Publishing App!

Soul Survivor, Moon Water Series, Book 1

Soul Protector, Moon Water Series, Book 2

Listen to the series on the Eleven Reader Publishing App!

COZY MYSTERIES (WRITING AS NYX HALLIWELL)

Sister Witches Of Raven Falls Mystery Series

Of Potions and Portents

Of Curses and Charms

Of Stars and Spells

Of Spirits and Superstition

Confessions of a Closet Medium Series

Pumpkins & Poltergeists

Magic & Mistletoe

Hearts & Haunts

Vows & Vengeance

Cupcakes & Corpses

Tea Leaves & Troubled Spirits

Haunted Honeymoon

Wedding Bells & Psychic Spells

Phantoms Are Forever

Skeletons & Scandals (featuring Cooking With Ghosts: Hauntingly Good Southern Recipes)

Murder & Marigolds (Coming Spring 2026)

Listen to the series on the Eleven Reader Publishing App!

For Nyx's haunted recipes, check out Cooking With Ghosts: Hauntingly Good Southern Recipes

Standalone Cozy Mystery

The Purrfectly Haunted Library

Sister Witches of Story Cove Series

Cinder

Belle

Snow

Ruby

Zelle

Sister Witches of Story Cove Complete Set

***

Witchy Candy Shop Mysteries

Tricks and Treats

Candy and Creeps

Gum and Ghouls

THRILLING ROMANTIC SUSPENSE & MYSTERIES

Don't want to miss a single release? Sign up for my newsletter at www.mistyevansbooks.com

Black Swan Division Romantic Thriller Series

Redeeming Meg

Tempting Tessa

Avenging Jessie

SEALs of Shadow Force Series

Fatal Truth

Fatal Honor

Fatal Courage

Fatal Love

Fatal Vision

Fatal Thrill

Risk

Listen to the series on the Eleven Reader Publishing App!

SEALS of Shadow Force Series: Spy Division

Man Hunt

Man Killer

Man Down

Covert Affairs

Covert Tactics

Covert Obsession

Listen to the series on the Eleven Reader Publishing App!

The SCVC Taskforce Series

Deadly Pursuit

Deadly Deception

Deadly Force

Deadly Intent

Deadly Affair, A SCVC Taskforce novella

Deadly Attraction

Deadly Secrets

Deadly Holiday, A SCVC Taskforce novella

Deadly Target

Deadly Rescue

Deadly Bounty

Deadly Betrayal

Deadly Threat

The Super Agent Series

Operation Sheba

Operation Paris

Operation Proof of Life

Operation Lost Princess

Operation Ambush

Operation Contraband

Operation Sleeping With the Enemy

Operation Heist

The Justice Team Series with Adrienne Giordano

Stealing Justice

Cheating Justice

Holiday Justice

Exposing Justice

Undercover Justice

Protecting Justice

Missing Justice

Defending Justice

Schock Sisters Mystery Series w/Adrienne Giordano

1st Shock

2nd Strike

3rd Tango

4th Silence

The Secret Ingredient Culinary Mystery Series

The Secret Ingredient, A Culinary Romantic Mystery with Bonus Recipes

The Secret Life of Cranberry Sauce, A Secret Ingredient Holiday Novella

VISIT MY STORE

Did you know you can buy directly from me? When you do, the retailer doesn't take a cut and I can pass on the savings to YOU!

https://mistyevansbooks.com/shop

Benefits:
> You can find ALL my books in one place
> SAVE money
> EARLY access to new releases
> Special Collections, Boxed eSets, and Limited Editions
> Support a small business (and support a dream!)

Why Buy Direct?
> When you purchase a book by your favorite author, electronic or print, on retailer platforms, the company keeps 30-70% of the sale, leaving the author with little to no profit (after the company deducts delivery fees, taxes, and other fees).

Buying directly from the author means that more goes to them so they can keep turning out stories for you. Every published story, every book, requires cover art, editing, and hours and hours of the author's time simply to create it. Not to mention overhead costs, such as websites, newsletters, writing software, graphics programs, advertising, taxes, etc.

In addition, one of the big-name retailers requires exclusivity, and all of them have terms of service and rules and regulations that make it challenging and time-consuming for an indie author to navigate the publishing world.

Most of us would MUCH rather spend our time creating more stories for YOU, rather than trying to jump through the hoops at the retailers. Buying direct from your favorite authors (where available) helps ensure that an author you love is not subject to unexplained account closures, withholding of royalties, censorship, and other issues that can affect their livelihood.

I've experienced ALL of these. By buying direct, you help put control of my work back in my hands - and I can continue to write more.

Either way, thank you for supporting me! I understand buying direct doesn't work for everyone and even if you use the retailers to buy my books, I appreciate you!

Happy reading,

Misty

https://mistyevansbooks.com/shop

MEET MISTY

USA TODAY Bestselling Author Misty Evans is celebrating her 100th published novel in 2025. She loves writing urban fantasy, paranormal romance, and mystery/suspense. Under her pen name, Nyx Halliwell, she also writes supernatural cozy mysteries.

When not reading or writing (which is most of the time), she enjoys music, movies, and hanging out with her husband, twin sons, and three spoiled rescue dogs. She's a crafter at heart and has far too many projects to finish.

Visit www.mistyevansbooks.com to check out her online store and sign up for her newsletter.

NOTE FROM MISTY

Thank you for reading this story! It is an honor and a privilege to write books for you. I'm an indie author, and every fan is important to me. I pour my heart into each story and do my best to bring you an escape from the real world.

Readers are the key to my success - not a traditional publishing deal (I've had four), an agent (I've had two), or a publicity team (yes, you guessed it, I've had several of those as well.)

Those of you who read my books, love my characters and worlds, and then tell others about them are the best of friends. I adore you and will keep writing if you keep reading!

If you'd like to learn about my other books, sales, and special promotions, please sign up for my newsletter at **www.mistyevansbooks.com**. You'll receive FREE series starters from me.

Support me directly (no retailer taking their cut), grab

special edition box sets, and get new releases before they are out at retailers by visiting my store **https://mistyevans books.com/shop**.

I have sales and offer NEW RELEASES early! Check it out.

Last but not least, if you enjoy clean, cozy mysteries, visit my pen name **www.nyxhalliwell.com** to see those books.

Thank you, and happy reading!
Misty

www.ingramcontent.com/pod-product-compliance
Lightning Source LLC
Chambersburg PA
CBHW031216020726
47499CB00002B/613